THE DEAD DROP

by

PETER JAMES CHILD

**Sequel to
THE DISPOSER**

Benbow Publications

© Copyright 2017 by Peter James Child

Peter James Child has asserted his right under the Copyright, Designs and Patents Act, 1988 to be identified as the author of this work.

All rights reserved. No part of this publication may be reproduced, stored in a retrieval system, or transmitted in any form or by any means, electronic, mechanical photocopying, recording or otherwise without the prior permission of the copyright holder.

Published in 2017 by Benbow Publications

British Library
Cataloguing in Publication Data.

ISBN: 978-1-908760-31-9

Printed by Lightning Source UK Ltd
Chapter House
Pitfield
Kiln Farm
Milton Keynes
MK11 3LW

First Edition

OTHER TITLES BY THE AUTHOR

THE DISPOSER

ERIC THE ROMANTIC
ERIC AND THE DIVORCEE
ERIC AND THE TWINS

THE MICHEL RONAY SERIES

MARSEILLE TAXI
AUGUST IN GRAMBOIS
CHRISTMAS IN MARSEILLE
CATASTROPHE IN LE TOUQUET
RETURN TO MARSEILLE

THE INSPECTOR HADLEY SERIES

THE TAVISTOCK SQUARE MURDERS
THE GOLD BULLION MURDERS
THE TOWER OF LONDON MURDERS
THE AMERICAN MURDERS
THE DIAMOND MURDERS
THE ROYAL RUSSIAN MURDERS
THE SATAN MURDERS
THE MEDICAL MURDERS
THE WESTMINSTER MURDERS
THE GIGOLO MURDERS
THE HOLY GRAIL MURDERS
THE DIPLOMAT MURDERS
THE MACABRE MURDERS
THE INGENIOUS MURDERS
THE FOREIGN OFFICE MURDERS

NON-FICTION

NOTES FOR GOOD DRIVERS
NOTES FOR COMPANY DRIVERS
VEHICLE PAINTER'S NOTES
VEHICLE FINE FINISHING
VEHICLE FABRICATIONS IN GRP

ACKNOWLEDGEMENTS

Once again, I wish to gratefully acknowledge the help and assistance given to me by Lucy Harpur, who edited this book. Thanks also to Sue Gresham, who formatted it and to Wendy Tobitt, for the splendid cover presentation. Without these talented and patient ladies this book would not have been possible.

Peter James Child

This book is dedicated to Dave and Paula Buller.

INTRODUCTION

After my good friend Roger Burton accidently killed his French mistress, Nicole, while they were playing sex games, I had reluctantly disposed of her lovely, naked body. This led to my involvement with Natasha, the nymphomaniac lover of Charles Macmillan; a Government Minister, who had also accidently killed a woman, in similar circumstances.

After I disposed of her body, I managed, with some difficulty, to extricate myself from this dangerous web of murder and sexual intrigue… a web spun by Natasha, Macmillan and his wealthy Russian friends, for the 'greater good.' I retired to my farm in Dorset… however, fate had other ideas, and soon I was contacted again by Natasha, closely followed by her 'friend,' a wealthy Chinese businessman, living in London.

The nightmare started once again, after he made me a financial offer I couldn't refuse… which was coupled with more than a hint of blackmail!

Characters and events portrayed in this book are fictional.

CHAPTER 1

IT STARTS AGAIN

I had retired from flying fast jets in the Royal Air Force, after twelve years of active service, and I had inherited a lovely, picturesque, arable farm in Dorset, from my late Uncle Ted. He also left me his Bentley, along with fifty thousand pounds… so, I believed I was set for a comfortable rural life.

I bought a Cessna 172 light aircraft, registration G-BNPO, call sign Golf Papa Oscar, which I flew for pleasure, from my farm strip. I met Louise, who became my lovely wife; within a year we'd had twins, Samantha and Scott, which made our life complete. Unbeknown to Louise, a year earlier, I'd become reluctantly involved in a dreadful situation, caused by my old school friend, Roger Burton. He'd accidently killed his French mistress, Nicole, while playing a sex game, which had resulted in me disposing of her naked body, by dropping it far out at sea, from my Cessna.

After that incident, I was contacted by Richard Templeton, and it was necessary for me to repeat the disposal service, after his wife Natasha and her lover, Charles Macmillan, a Government Minister, accidently killed a Lithuanian girl, during a sex game. From then on, I became involved with Macmillan and his team, by disposing of their 'necessary dead', until Macmillan was shot and killed outside his London home. When the police had completed their inquiries, with no results, my comfortable life resumed once more… until the phone call that would shatter everything!

It was soon after Louise and I returned from our holiday with the twins, when Natasha Templeton phoned me. It was a shock, as I believed that she'd left the country more than a year ago, with Igor, her Russian lover. I was walking along the strip by the top meadow, with my farm manager Bob Williams, discussing the expected wheat yield later in the year, when my mobile rang… I ignored it for a moment, but it persisted…

'Hello.'

1

'Hello, Peter... Peter Cavendish? Do you remember me?' Natasha asked.

I shivered, as I remembered escaping from the crazy, semi-naked nymphomaniac, while she was still strapped on the swing in her pleasure room... it was just before I met Charles Macmillan, in the hallway of the Templeton's house, on that fateful night.

'Natasha...?'

'...So, you do remember me!'

'How could I ever forget you?' I asked anxiously... wondering what was coming next.

'I need to see you again,' she purred.

'I'm afraid that's impossible, Natasha...'

'...Why?' she interrupted.

'...Because I'm married now... with two children, so...'

'It is important, Peter,' she interrupted firmly.

'Natasha...'

'...Just say you'll see me... I promise it won't take long, and it's in your best interests,' she persisted.

'No, Natasha, I can't get involved with you...'

'...So, do you want me to come down to your farm then?'

'No... please don't...'

'...Because I will, if you won't meet me...'

'Please, Natasha,' I interrupted.

'...Then, you must come and meet me, Peter... it is very important,' she said, firmly.

I gave in... mainly because I knew I had no other option... and God only knows what trouble she would cause if she arrived unexpectedly... Louise would have a fit!

I took a deep breath and said, 'alright... okay...so, where are you now, Natasha?'

'I've moved to Abingdon, near Oxford and...'

'Well, I'm not coming to your house!' I interrupted.

'...Why ever not?'

'You know what happened in Wallingford,' I replied, firmly.

'So, what do you suggest then?'

'We meet somewhere in public... a pub or a hotel,' I replied.

'Alright... how about we meet at midday tomorrow, at the Crown in Abingdon? It's in Bridge Street... it's a nice hotel...

and, you can buy me lunch!'

'I can't meet you tomorrow because I'm busy, but I can make it on Wednesday,' I replied.

'Okay... that's a date... and, make sure you come...bye, Peter.'

'Bye, Natasha,' I whispered, and wondered, 'what the hell am I getting into now?'

'Anything wrong, boss?' asked Bob.

'No, nothing I can't handle, Bob,' I replied, but thought, 'I hope... God help me!'

I remained in a subdued mood for the rest of the day, and spent a restless night worrying about bloody Natasha Templeton, and what she could possibly have in mind. I knew from bitter, past experience that it wouldn't be anything good, but resolved to face it head on... whatever it was. I had one crumb of comfort that sprang to mind, in the middle of the night... after I'd discovered what sex-mad Natasha wanted, I would visit my wealthy Aunt Paula, to discuss the situation and take her advice.

Paula lived in Yarnton, near Oxford. She had helped me previously with money and suggestions... which enabled me to safely navigate around the dangerous situations, caused by Charles Macmillan and his wealthy murderous Russian friends, when disposing of dead bodies!

My good friend Roger Burton, who, as I've already said, accidently killed his French mistress, Nicole, believed I'd buried her on my farm. I had, in fact, taken off from my farm strip in my Cessna, with Nicole's body on board. I'd then dumped her far out in the Atlantic, from 2,000 feet... which was an easy task for me, after flying jets in the RAF... I'd, subsequently, followed the same procedure with all the other dead females. I was certain that nobody would ever know what had happened to these poor young women, and if the police suspected me of any involvement in their disappearance, they could dig up the whole farm and find nothing that would implicate me in their disposal.

Wednesday dawned, and I told Louise over breakfast that I intended to visit Paula, after meeting an old friend in Abingdon. My wife was too busy feeding our growing twins, to pay much attention, or ask any awkward questions... which was a relief!

'Give Paula my love,' Louise said, as she spooned cereal into Scott.

'...Of course, darling.'

'...And, ask her when she's coming down to see us,' she said, as Samantha spat her cereal all over the table.

'I will,' I replied, with a smile, while thinking, *my children are so lovely, but incredibly messy!*

It was just before ten when I set off in the Bentley, to meet the troublesome Natasha. During the whole journey my mind was in a constant whirl of unanswered questions. *Was Igor, her demanding Russian lover, still with her?* I thought. *Did he murder Charles Macmillan outside his London home, a year ago?* And, *did Mrs Lovensky, who shot their maid, when she caught her in the bath with her husband, know who killed Macmillan?* And, *who was Mr Tolstoy?* A few weeks later, I had flown him to France with Mrs Lovensky, so *did he play any part in the murder of Macmillan?* What a terrible web of murder and intrigue I had reluctantly become involved in... and, it was all because of Roger! He should have known better, being a barrister at the Criminal Bar... but, I suppose, the line between good and bad behaviour becomes blurred over time, in that line of work. *Dear God, so many questions for Natasha to answer...* I hoped.

I arrived in Abingdon just before midday. I found the Crown Hotel in Bridge Street, and parked nearby. As soon as I entered the picturesque, old coaching inn, I noticed Natasha sitting in the reception. She stood to greet me, with a smile, and I gave a nod, before walking over to her.

'Peter, how are you, darling? You do look well,' she purred, as she held out her hand to me. I took it, before she quickly kissed me on the cheek, and I caught the scent of her exotic perfume.

'...And you're as lovely as usual, Natasha,' I replied... and, meant it. She looked beautiful; her lovely face was perfectly made up, to enhance her soulful brown eyes, and her lustrous, dark hair, was swept up into an elegant pleat.

'Thank you, darling… I do my best,' she smiled.

'…And, it shows… now, what's this all about?'

'Aren't you going to buy me a drink first?'

'…Of course…'

'Then we can have lunch, and I'll tell you all about it, darling.'

Natasha led me through to the bar; she seemed to know her way. I ordered a gin and tonic for her, while I had a glass of orange… as I wanted to keep all my wits about me. We sat in a corner, touched glasses, and said, 'cheers!' I was about to start asking her questions, when a waiter appeared, asking, 'are you having lunch today, sir?'

'Yes please,' I replied, and he handed us the menus, saying, 'come through whenever you're ready, sir.'

'Thank you,' and, when he was out of earshot, I said, 'now, I have a lot of questions…'

'I'm sure you have, darling,' she interrupted, then continued, as she glanced at the menu, '…but we must eat first… let's see what we'll have for lunch… the poached salmon is always divine here.'

'So, I presume this is your local?'

'Yes… but, only for lunch, darling.'

'How nice,' I said, in a sarcastic tone, thinking, *so this is where you come to pick up men?* How wrong I was!

'So, I think I'll have the salmon… with extra salad… what are you having, darling?'

I glanced at the menu, and chose the fillet steak, before asking, 'tell me, Natasha… why did you want to see me again?'

She looked concerned, while she gathered her thoughts, and I wondered what was coming next. She leaned slowly towards me, and replied in a whisper, 'I think you're in real danger of having to start burying bodies on your farm again...'

'Oh bloody hell!'

'…And, I had to warn you, darling… it's the very least I could do.'

'Is it your Russian friend, Igor, doing the killing?'

'Oh no, darling, that bastard left me stranded in Paris a year ago, without any money whatsoever, and went back to his bloody wife and children, in Moscow!' she replied angrily.

'…Who then?'

'…I don't really know for sure,' she replied.

'For God's sake, Natasha… stop playing games!'

'I'm not…'

'I think you only wanted us to meet, so you could practice your crazy sexual fantasies on me again!' I interrupted.

'No… that's not true!'

'…What then?' I asked angrily.

'Let me tell you, Peter… I really don't need you anymore…'

'…Well, that's fine by me!'

'I have all the attention I need now, from two lovely young men… there's Tim, who's a farmer, and Chris, who works at the bank in Oxford, where I have my account,' she replied, firmly. I felt relieved that she wasn't going to make any sexual demands on me.

She droned on about them being close friends from school, and Rugby players… so fit and strong, while being highly imaginative, when it came to giving her complete and total sexual satisfaction. Natasha finally said, with a glint in her eye, 'and after they've eventually finished me off, I feel quite exhausted, darling… especially when they've both had me together!' which resulted in my imagination running riot!

I paused for a moment, to clear my mind of the vision of Natasha being pounded, without mercy, in every possible position, into a state of sublime ecstasy, by these two boisterous young men, before asking, 'so what makes you think I'm in danger of having to dispose of bodies again?'

'…Well, I know Charles told several people about his 'team of experts,' who were ready to do anything for the 'greater good' of the country… which included disposing of those he called, 'the necessary dead', and your name often came up in conversation,' she replied.

'…Oh dear God,' I whispered.

'…And, last Sunday, I got a call from Andrew… he was one of Charles' team. He told me that someone had been making enquiries about the members of the team,' she said, anxiously.

'...Do you know who?'

'...No... and, neither does Andrew.'

'Does he not have the remotest idea who this person might be?'

'I don't think so.'

'Well, what a bloody mess!'

'...But, Charles did tell me about several of his acquaintances, and one I do remember was a Chinese businessman called, Lu something-or-other. He was, supposedly, ruthless and involved in supplying the Chinese Government with technical know-how about American missiles,' she replied.

'...And, why should he be interested in me?'

'I don't know that he is, darling... but his killer might be.'

'...Is he dead?'

'I don't know if he is or not, but he bought a home in London, after hurriedly leaving China, under a cloud. Charles said he must have some powerful enemies, so someone must want him dead,' she replied.

'Did Charles ever say who that might be?'

'No... and, I honestly don't know, darling,' she replied, then asked brightly, 'shall we go into lunch?'

Realising that she knew very little, I nodded, finished my drink, and followed her through to the restaurant, where we were greeted and shown to a table in the corner.

After we had ordered our meals, I was anxious to know more about this mysterious Chinaman.

'So, tell me... what else do you know about this Mr Lu?'

'Not much... I only met him a few times, when Charles brought him to our house in Wallingford.'

'...I suppose for some action in your pleasure room?'

'Yes, he liked to watch,' she replied, with a coy smile.

'...How satisfying for him.'

All through our lunch, I persistently asked questions about the Russians and the present situation, but Natasha was more than vague with her answers. She told me that the other men Charles mentioned were American, Saudi Arabian, Romanian or Italian...

all of whom now lived in London. She couldn't remember any names, but said that Charles thought some might be employed by their Governments, who would wish to see Mr Lu dead, for some obscure reason.

My mind was sick with fear, I wondered what would happen next…and, who would contact me… if, or when, Mr Lu had been murdered… and, all just as I was happily settled with my lovely wife Louise and the twins!

As we sipped coffee, I asked Natasha for her address and phone number, which she willingly gave me, and she asked, in anticipation, 'so are you going to come and see me, or just call, darling?'

'I'll call you, Natasha… in case I need more information about the foreigners… that is, if you can remember anything… and, please give me Andrew's phone number.'

'I don't know it… Charles kept everything secret from me… he always said it was best that I never knew anything.'

'Dear God,' I whispered, realising another door had closed, on any hope of discovering the identity of who might be involved.

Natasha smiled, and said, 'well it's a shame you won't come and see me… but, don't phone in the evening… afternoons are better, as Tim and Chris usually come to visit me most evenings, and I don't want to be disturbed,' and I thought, *I'm not surprised!*

After taking a moment to clear my mind, again, of Natasha with the fit, young Rugby players, I said firmly, 'well, please ask Andrew to phone me, if he calls you again.'

'Of course I will, darling.'

We said our 'goodbyes' outside the hotel, and I thanked Natasha for the warning, telling her that I would keep in touch. She gave me a lingering kiss on the cheek, and waved to me as I crossed the road, to the car park. I sat in the Bentley and contemplated the impending disastrous situation for a while, before I phoned Aunt Paula.

Paula had married my Uncle Richard, mother's younger brother, years ago, but it was obvious from the start that they were not well matched, and their marriage fell apart three years later. After they were divorced, Richard immigrated to Australia, while Paula bought a small flat in Oxford, and started a business called, 'Executive Excellence.' She recruited graduates and dons from the universities, placing them into key positions within international companies, in the USA, Hong Kong, China and Germany. She was extremely successful and soon very wealthy.

Paula bought a large, detached, Georgian house in the village of Yarnton, near Oxford, and she always changed her BMW saloon each year, for the latest model. She had many admirers, some of whom had proposed to her, but she always kept the relationships brief, saying, 'I don't intend to marry again... and, I'm pleased to say, that I wasn't married for long enough the first time, to do any permanent damage!'

After selling her lucrative business a year ago, to one of her clients, Steven; a seriously wealthy Wall Street trader, she went on a world cruise. Paula is now one of the idle rich, she's also godmother to the twins, and generous to a fault, to Louise and myself!

Paula was my rock when I was in the darkest of places, over a year ago; when I began dumping dead females from my Cessna, out in the Atlantic. She guided me through the sexual demands of Natasha; as well as Charles Macmillan's web of deadly intrigue and murder. I thought that was all behind me, and was now a history, which would never be repeated... how wrong I was!

After phoning Paula, I drove up to Yarnton and was greeted by my attractive, voluptuous, sexy, smiling, aunt, who kissed me firmly on the lips, as she hugged me.

'Oh, it's so good to see you, Peter...'

'...Likewise, Aunt.'

'Come through to the kitchen, and have some tea, while you tell me all your news.'

'Thanks,' I replied, before following on to her spacious, well-appointed kitchen.

Clicking on the kettle, she asked, 'so, how is Louise... and the babes?'

'They're all well, thanks... Louise sends her love, and asks when are you coming down to visit?'

'…Well, now I've sold the business and finished cruising for a while, my time's my own… so, you just say when, darling.'

'I'll get Louise to give you a call, and you two can make arrangements.'

'Lovely… now, is your visit a social one, or is there something else?'

'Oh, you know me so well, Paula!'

'I certainly do,' she replied, as she poured hot water into the teapot.

I paused for a moment, to gather my thoughts, and said, 'I've been contacted by Natasha again…'

Paula stopped instantly, and asked, wide eyed, 'not nympho Natasha?'

'Yes… the very same!'

'Dear God, what does she want? Other than the obvious, that is!'

'She said she wanted to warn me, that I might be called upon, to dispose of more bodies,' I replied.

'Oh my God… I thought that was all well and truly behind you, darling.'

'…So did I.'

'…Well, tell me everything,' she said, as she sat at the table and poured the tea. I told Paula, in detail, what Natasha had said, and when I'd finished, she asked, 'so, you don't know who this Mr Lu is, or who might want him dead?'

'No… so, you can take your pick from the foreigners, living in London, that Macmillan talked to about his team of experts, who could dispose of the 'necessary dead,' I replied.

'What a dreadful world,' she said, with a sigh.

'…So, what do you advise me to do?'

'My first instinct is that you should do nothing… nothing at all… Natasha may be playing some game with you, out of revenge…or, what she told you may have an element of truth in it, but we'll cross that bridge when we come to it… after someone phones you, darling,' she replied, with a smile.

I sighed and said, 'what a dreadful mess!'

'Don't worry, this Andrew may be able to help, and we'll get through it somehow.'

'I bloody well hope so!'

'…And, if someone phones you, and you find yourself reluctantly, once more, in this dangerous, murderous swamp, then you must tell Louise.'

'…Tell Louise?'

'…Yes, you must, darling.'

'I couldn't possibly do that!'

'…But, how can you possibly manage to keep it from her, this time? She lives with you now!'

'I don't know, but I'll have to try,' I replied.

'How on earth would you explain your early morning flights?'

'I'll think of something… I'll have to!'

'Well, it's obvious you're not thinking clearly…'

'That's possibly true!' I interrupted.

'If you start disposing of dead bodies into the Atlantic, from your little plane, Louise will know immediately, darling… she's a very smart woman, and you have to tell her…'

'…But, she'll leave me… and, take the twins with her!'

'No, she won't…'

'Paula… believe me…she will!'

'…Louise is one of the most loyal women I've ever met… she will always stand by you, no matter what… and, if you tell her the truth, then she'll help you… just as I will,' Paula said, firmly.

My confused mind was once more in a whirl, and I didn't know what to think for the best.

We sat and talked for quite some time, and I gradually felt comforted by Paula's calm, serene approach to my difficult situation. Eventually, we said 'goodbye,' with hugs and long kisses; promising to keep in touch, before I climbed into the Bentley and headed home, to wait for Andrew to contact me… or the dreaded phone call, from a dangerous stranger.

Arriving home, I told Louise about Paula and her proposed visit, at any time, but never mentioned the meeting with Natasha. She didn't ask about my friend, in Abingdon, choosing to regale me about the twin's exploits… who, it seemed, had been more than a handful that day!

I needed some time to think, so decided to fly over to the nearby flying club, at West Compton... I'd have a chat with Alan Watkins, the chief instructor, who had taught Louise to fly... and probably call in to see Phil Green, in the Control Tower... then I would refuel Papa Oscar, before flying along the coast, towards Weymouth. I can always relax and think positively when I'm in control of an aircraft, as it's a comfortable, private place, and flying is second-nature to me.

Leaving the house, I walked the short distance, in the late afternoon sun, out to my smart little Cessna; parked at the top of the strip. I glanced at the windsock, for the wind direction, which was a gentle southerly, and then I carried out the ground checks, before climbing aboard. After starting the engine, I checked the instruments, called the control tower, for clearance, released the brakes, and then throttled up. Within a few hundred yards, I reached the take-off speed and eased Papa Oscar into the clear blue sky. It only took a few minutes to fly, at low level, to the airfield, where Phil gave me landing instructions, before I touched down. After parking near the tower, I went up and paid the landing fee, to Phil.

'You look a little bit weary today, Peter.'

'Do I?'

'Yes... so, what have you been up to, I wonder?' Phil asked, with a grin, before he gave taxi clearance to a Piper Cherokee.

I thought, *if only you knew!* But, replied, lamely, '...just been a bit busy with the farm lately.'

'Well, don't let it get in the way of your flying!' he replied, jovially.

'...I won't... bye for now, Phil,' I replied, with a smile, and left the tower. As I descended the stairs, I decided not to find Alan, for a chat, after all, as I was no longer in the mood for polite conversation... I just needed to re-fuel Papa Oscar, and take to the air.

My flight along the sunlit coast was restful, and I felt much more relaxed when I landed back at the farm.

In the evening, Louise cooked a lovely meal, and after we'd put the children to bed, we sat and talked, occasionally watching the television, before we went up to bed ourselves. As I lay on my back, thinking about the meeting with Natasha and Paula, Louise suddenly lifted herself up on her elbow, put her hand to the side of my face, turned it towards her, and said, as she peered into my eyes, 'so, tell me all about this friend of yours, that you met in Abingdon.' Women are so bloody curious! They just have to know everything... they *need* to know everything... they *will* eventually know everything...so, any resistance is futile!

I took a deep breath and, remembering what Paula had said, replied truthfully, 'her name is Natasha Templeton...'

'...Well, I knew it would be a woman,' Louise interrupted, with a sigh.

'...And she was the mistress of Charles Macmillan...'

'...The Minister who was murdered last year?'

'Yes...'

'So, why did she want to see you? Or was it the other way around?' she asked, in a suspicious tone.

'No, it wasn't... she bloody wanted to see me!'

'...What for?'

'She had a phone call from some chap called Andrew, who told her that someone had been contacting Macmillan's old staff...'

'...And?'

'Do you remember when I flew over to Le Touquet last year... before we were married?'

'Yes... and, I thought it was all a bit suspicious at the time,' she replied.

'Well, I took two of Macmillan's Russian friends over there...'

'Why?'

'...Because he asked me to.'

'...And does this *Natasha* person think you'll be asked to fly other people to France?'

'She said it's a possibility.'

'Dear God, Peter...whatever are you mixed up in?'

'I really don't know.'

'What do you mean "you don't know" were you a member of Macmillan's staff?'

'No... well, not in so many words... it's a long story...'

'I'm tired, but I'm listening... so, you'd better start near the end,' she said, with a sigh.

'Okay... I had a call from a chap called Richard Templeton, who asked to see me on a business matter...'

'...And that's when you met Natasha?' Louise interrupted.

'Yes... '

'...And, what was the business?'

I took a deep breath and decided to tell her a half-truth; leaving the sordid details until much later... I always believe that one shock at a time is preferable, don't you?

'Templeton asked me about flying a special person out from here.'

'From our farm?' she asked, in disbelief... I hadn't the heart to tell her the special person was a dead Lithuanian girl, who'd been strangled during a sex game, with Natasha and Macmillan.

'Yes.'

'...And did you do it?'

'Yes.'

'Where did you take her?'

'Does it matter?'

'Yes it does,' she replied... do you see what I mean about curious women?

'Well, that's a secret for the time being... but, I promise to tell you later.'

'...Hmm.'

'...Sometime after that, I met Macmillan at the Templeton's...'

'...And you became one of his team?'

'...Only at the very edge... really, I was more a sort of a 'hanger-on.' I was only needed occasionally, to fly people out of the country.'

'...So, who else is involved in all this?'

'...Well, actually, Roger started it...'

'I thought he'd be mixed up in this somehow!'

'You're right as usual, darling,' I replied... at that moment, one of the twins woke and started to cry.

Louise sighed, and said, 'that sounds like Samantha...you'd better go, because she settles quicker for you.'

'Yes, of course... you get some rest, darling ... you've had a busy day.'

Louise nodded, lay back with a sigh, and closed her eyes. I felt relieved that the questioning was over for tonight, but knew Louise would eventually want more answers. I decided, as I held Samantha in my arms, rocking her gently, that I would tell Louise everything... the whole dreadful story... but, it would have to wait for the right time.

The next morning passed without any further inquisition... and the next. In fact, Louise was far too busy with the twins to pay much attention to my past adventures, which suited me just fine. The following days slipped by without a phone call from Andrew or Mr Lu, or his killer, and I thought that Natasha was probably playing mind games with me... which was not unknown! I started to relax again, and got on with running the farm, with Bob... then, one night, a week later, came the dreaded call!

CHAPTER 2

THE CALL

I was sitting in my study, just after eight in the evening, checking my bank statement, when my mobile rang...

'Hello'

'Is that Mr Cavendish?' asked the caller, in a strange accent, and my blood ran ice cold.

'Who's this?'

'...I presume you are Peter Cavendish?'

'Yes, I am... now; tell me... who are you?'

'My name is Lu Ming...'

'What's this all about? And how did you get my number?' I interrupted, anxiously.

'Patience, Mr Cavendish... I will reveal everything to you when we meet.'

'Oh, I don't think so!'

'Ah, yes... believe me, Mr Cavendish... we will meet very soon,' he whispered, in a menacing tone.

'You may think so, Mr Lu... or whoever you are... but...'

'Mr Cavendish, let me be direct!' he interrupted, and I waited patiently for him to continue, whilst thinking desperately how I could rid myself of this unwanted caller.

'I know that you were part of the late Charles Macmillan's team of experts, who could be called upon in times of... shall we say *need?*'

'Well, you've been utterly misinformed, sir, because I'm a farmer,' I said, firmly.

'Ah, you are now, but you were a pilot in the Royal Air Force, and...'

'...Indeed I was, sir, but I had nothing to do with Charles Macmillan, who, as I'm sure you know, was shot dead outside his London home,' I interrupted.

'Yes, that was very regrettable...'

'...And, did you have anything to do with that?' I asked, now going on the offensive.

'No, Charles was my good friend, who helped me when I first moved to London.'

'Well, judging by the number of people he helped to enter the country, as the Border Agency Minister, everyone was his friend... well, except for one person... who unfortunately killed him!'

'Yes...'

'...So, why are you contacting me?' I interrupted.

'I've told you...'

'No you haven't... you said I was part of his team, which is far from the truth!'

'Charles told me that you quickly disposed of troublesome females, and flew his Russian friends to France.'

'Did he now?' I asked, as I began to sweat.

'So, I believe you were part of his team... and, now I want to meet you, so we can discuss my needs,' he said ominously.

'I'm afraid that's not possible...'

'Mr Cavendish, you have a choice before you... either meet me in London, or very soon the police will be digging up your farm, looking for bodies!'

I trembled inside and thought, *what a bastard Macmillan was, telling all and sundry about my disposal activities for him,* but I had no choice, and reluctantly asked, with a sigh, 'so where and when?'

'Come to my house, in Grosvenor Square, tomorrow morning, say at about eleven... and, be sure you come, Mr Cavendish,' he replied in a threatening tone.

'I'll be there... what's the number?'

'I live at number forty-two... just near the American Embassy... until tomorrow then.'

'Goodbye, Mr Lu Ming,' I said, and flung my mobile down on the desk.

I sat thinking for a while, and decided that I had to tell Louise about this trip to London, to meet the mysterious Oriental.

Louise was sitting at the kitchen table. Glancing up from her cookery book, she said, 'fancy some coffee?'

'Yes, why not... I could do with something.'

She looked at me curiously for a moment, and then asked, 'whatever's the matter, darling?'

I sighed, sat down opposite her, and replied, 'I've just had a phone call from a Mr Lu Ming…'

'…And what the hell did he want?' she interrupted.

'…To see me, in London, tomorrow morning, at eleven.'

'…And, are you going?'

'I don't think I have much choice.'

'Dear God, whatever are you involved in?'

'I really don't know at the moment, but I'll find out tomorrow,' I replied, and Louise rolled her eyes.

'Well, whatever he wants, just tell him "no".'

'It might not be that easy.'

Louise hesitated for a moment, then said, 'well, on second thoughts, I suppose you'd better go, otherwise you'll never find out what he wants, will you?' and, I just nodded.

Following another restless night, I showered early and made breakfast, while Louise took care of the twins. After saying 'goodbye' to my wife and the babes, I set off in the Bentley, which wafted me effortlessly up the motorway, to London. As it was a Sunday morning, I managed to park close to the American Embassy and walked along to number forty-two; where I rang the bell and waited. The door was eventually opened by a beautiful young Chinese woman, who looked angelic, with a smiling face, and said, 'good morning, sir.'

'Good morning… I'm Peter Cavendish, and I'm here to see Mr Lu Ming.'

'Yes, sir, he's expecting you… please come in,' she said, as she stood back to allow me to enter the spacious, well-furnished hallway.

'Thank you.'

'Please wait here,' she said, before entering ornate double doors, which she closed behind her. I heard voices before she re-appeared, and said, 'Mr Ming will see you now, sir.'

'Thank you,' I replied, gave a nod and entered the room, which was obviously a study… behind a large, ostentatious desk, emblazoned with curled golden dragons, stood Mr Lu Ming. I scrutinised the vertically-challenged, slightly-built Chinaman, as he said, 'ah, good morning, Mr Cavendish... so glad you came.'

'Good morning.'

'Please be seated... may I offer you some tea?' he asked, with a smile... but, I didn't like all this carefully rehearsed politeness, from a menacing stranger... it usually precedes something unpleasant!

'Thank you.'

He nodded, pushed a button somewhere under his desk, and moments later the maid reappeared. He gave her an instruction in Cantonese, before she nodded and left.

I decided to remain silent, trying to put this man under some pressure, but he just stared back at me, from his black leather executive chair; which was also heavily emblazoned with golden dragons. We sat looking at each other, and I thought *the first one to speak is lost*... so, I waited.

'Mr Cavendish... you're quite a difficult man to read,' Mr Ming said, with a curious smile; expecting some response, but I remained silent. I was obviously getting under his shiny, jaundiced skin, and it pleased me.

'I expect you're wondering why I sent for you?' he asked, but I remained silent, and just stared at him.

'I have a problem... probably more than one, and I believe you can help me,' he said firmly, staring at me, with malice in his dark, beady eyes. I raised my eyebrows and waited.

'Mr Cavendish...'

'What the hell do you really want with me?' I interrupted, in a whisper through clenched teeth, and he smiled, as the doors behind me opened, and the girl appeared with the tea. As she placed the tray on his desk, he spoke again in Cantonese; she nodded, and poured the tea into small, delicate porcelain cups. After giving a little bow, she left the study.

'Milk? Sugar?' he asked, and I shook my head at both. He picked up his cup, I did likewise, and after he had taken a sip, he said, 'I need your special help, Mr Cavendish... and I will ensure that you are rewarded very handsomely.'

'...How handsomely?'

'Well that all depends…'

'I don't work for anyone on *all depends,*' I interrupted.

He sighed and replied, 'alright then… I'll give you fifty thousand pounds, in cash, every time you help me…'

'Help you what?' I interrupted.

'Dispose of the necessary dead… as Charles used to say…'

'For the greater good?'

'Precisely.'

'And who are these dead?' I asked, thinking that, 'fifty thousand in cash sounded attractive,' but I was determined that I wasn't getting into any murderous undertakings with him.

'Let me begin at the beginning… I've been a very successful businessman in Beijing, and over the years I've accumulated a lot of money. I prudently placed this in banks in Hong Kong, where I have another home… in Switzerland, Panama, the Cayman Islands, Bermuda, and several other countries… where it's possible to do so without attracting too much attention, from the authorities.'

'I see… and, now what?'

'The Chinese Government are not too happy with me… and, for various other reasons, which need not concern you, I believe they want me dead!'

'I'm not surprised.'

'I'm sure you're not, Mr Cavendish, but my life is precious to me.'

'…As mine is to me…'

He nodded, and continued, 'so, I believe, that there are already agents of the Chinese Government, here in London, ready to assassinate me.'

'…And, I presume you intend to kill them first?'

'Yes, I do intend to strike first… Charles always said you were a man who quickly grasped the situation,' he said, with a smile.

'That's probably true… and you want me to dispose of these necessary dead?'

'Of course… and, you must ensure they are never found… and, I will make certain that the Beijing Government think their agents have defected to the west, and are now in hiding.'

'What makes you think the top brass in Beijing will believe

you?'

'That's easy... because, they know that the west is very attractive to the poorly-paid Chinese; who are employed by the state... there is easy money to be made here, added luxuries and low morals,' he said triumphantly.

I stared at him, and said, 'well, Mr Ming... you can count me out!'

'What?' he asked, incredulously, as he sat forward in his chair, and glared at me.

'You heard... I'm not getting involved with you or your murderous plans.'

'You'll regret this, you foolish man!'

'...Possibly.'

'I'll see to it that you end up in prison!'

'We'll have to see about that, won't we?'

'Mr Cavendish... if you refuse to help me, then I will inform certain contacts of mine that you are hiding bodies on your farm!'

'Please do,' I countered with a smile.

'Then the police will be swarming over every inch of your land, and you will be arrested for certain!'

'You can't blackmail me.'

'Ah... now I see... judging by your confidence, I can safely assume that the bodies aren't buried at the farm... so, you've disposed of them elsewhere!' he said, triumphantly. That touched a nerve, and I was about to reply, when I heard the doors behind me open.

Ming glanced up, smiled and said, 'ah, Leisha my love, come and meet Mr Cavendish... this is my wife, Leisha.'

I stood up and turned to face a beautiful young woman, who held out her hand and purred, 'Mr Cavendish... I'm so pleased to meet you.'

'How do you do, Mrs Ming?' I replied, as I gently took her hand and thought, 'Lu Ming, you lucky bastard!' I was mesmerised by her appearance... she was taller and much younger than her husband, and part Chinese, while I guessed the other part was probably, elegant, slim Malay... she was stunningly beautiful. Leisha had lustrous black hair, which had been gently rolled back in waves and tied with a red bow, to reveal her face, with its flawless olive complexion and beautiful, penetrating, brown eyes. She had a serene, but sultry look about her, which was most attractive. She was dressed in a pure white, fitted dress, which showed off her elegant and well-proportioned figure.

Leisha smiled, and said to her husband, 'so, have you finished your business yet, darling?'

'Almost,' he replied, and turning to me, she asked, 'you will stay for lunch, Mr Cavendish, won't you?' How could I possibly resist? So replied, 'I'd be delighted to, Mrs Ming.'

'I'm so pleased… come through when you're ready,' she said, with a smile, before leaving the study.

I resumed my seat, looked at Ming, who said with a smile, 'now please let us not argue, Mr Cavendish… it's pointless… I need your help, so please consider the dangerous situation that affects us both.' Before I could reply, he continued, 'now let's go and enjoy lunch with my wife, while you consider your future choice… of either prison, or considerable financial gains.'

I gave a nod, followed him out of the study and across the hallway, to the dining room, where, laid out on an elegant table, was enough food, in gold rimmed dishes, to feed the five thousand. Mrs Ming stood on one side of the table and, with a smile, waved me to sit opposite, while her husband sat at the head in a large ornate chair.

I surveyed the food laid out before us, and could see some dishes I recognised, like sweet and sour pork, kung pao chicken, chow mein and egg fried rice, but I didn't recognise any of the other foods on offer.

'Pleased help yourself, Mr Cavendish,' said Ming, with a smile.

'Well, I think I'm spoilt for choice,' I replied, glancing around at the dishes.

'Then, let me help you,' said Leisha.

'Thank you.'

Leisha pointed out various dishes, while informing me what they were, as Ming filled his bowl, and began to eat with chopsticks. I chose egg fried rice with sweet and sour pork, to begin, and, using a spoon, began to eat the delicious food. After I had finished my first course, I tried various dishes that Leisha recommended, and was pleased that I'd followed her advice.

When the meal was over, and tea had been served by the maid, Leisha looked at me anxiously, and said, 'my husband tells me that he is now in great danger from the Government in Beijing, and you are a brave man, who can help him... so, will you help him, Mr Cavendish?'

I looked into her lovely brown eyes, and felt that I couldn't resist her desperate appeal for my help, so, with my conscience screaming not to get involved, I replied, 'I'll do whatever I can to help your husband, Mrs Ming.'

'Oh, thank you, thank you so much... I do appreciate your kindness,' she said, as tears coursed down her perfect cheeks. I glanced at Ming, as his wife wiped away her tears with a handkerchief, while he smiled, saying, 'thank you, Mr Cavendish,' and I nodded.

We returned to the study to discuss the imminently dangerous situation, that Lu Ming feared, and I then left the house in Grosvenor Square, feeling quite uneasy. On the journey back to the farm, I was trying to decide what I should do next, when Lu Ming phoned me, with instructions for the first disposal. I decided that I would tell Louise everything... every damnable thing!

I parked the Bentley, went into the house, and found Louise on the floor in the drawing room, playing with the children.

She looked up, and asked, 'well, how did it go?' but, before I could answer, my mobile rang and I hoped it wasn't Mr Lu Ming.

'Hello.'

'Hello, Peter... Roger here... how are you, old sport?'

'Well, I think... but, you sound on top form,' I replied.

'I am, dear boy... I'm about to become a father!'

'Congratulations, well done... and how is Naomi?'

'She's okay... apart from a bit of morning sickness, you know.'

'That's to be expected... so, when is the baby due?'

'I don't know for sure, but I guess in about seven months, or so,' he replied, as Louise waved at me and mouthed, 'who is it?' I replied in a whisper, 'Roger,' and, she raised her eyebrows.

'So, the wife and I wondered if we could take a break, and visit you for a bit of country air, before she gets too fat to move,' said Roger, with a chuckle.

'Of course... it would be good to see you both...when do you plan to come down?'

'Next Friday, and stay for the weekend, if that's okay with you,' he replied.

'That'll be fine Roger... Louise and I will look forward to it.'

'Good... until Friday then,' he said.

'Until Friday... bye, Roger.'

'Bye.'

I looked at Louise, and said, 'they're coming down next Friday, and staying for the weekend.'

'Well, I just hope they don't have such long faces this time.'

'They'll be okay... Roger has been more settled recently, and seems quite happy since he married Naomi... and now they're having a baby.'

'Hmm... I wonder if he really is happy about that... in my experience men who get divorced and marry their mistresses in a hurry, always end up regretting it.'

'You're just being cynical,' I replied, while thinking that now Roger was to become a father, had he said farewell to his other mistress? He had been seeing Kate during his marriage to Anne, and had continued after they were divorced... I wondered if he'd been faithful in his marriage to Naomi... but, I'd bet my life he hadn't! If that was the case, then more female trouble was certainly in store for him!

Louise brought me back to reality, saying, 'I'm being truthful... now, how did you get on with the Chinese businessman?'

I told Louise everything that had happened at Lu Ming's home, but left out the intended disposal of his enemies... I thought it best to leave that unpleasantness until another, more appropriate time.

'So, what exactly does this Mr Lu Ming want you to do?'

'Well, just fly people around, when he asks me to,' I replied.

'Where to?'

'I don't know, darling, until he tells me.'
'Aren't you worried about getting mixed up in all this?'
'Of course I am, but I'll just have to see what develops.'
'Yes, I suppose we'll have to wait and see,' she said as Scott made a grab at Samantha's hair, which made her scream; abruptly ending our conversation.

Monday and Tuesday passed without any further discussions about Mr Lu Ming, while I continued to ponder if I should tell Louise the whole dreadful story. I was still undecided whether or not to tell her, but remembering what Paula had said, I thought it best that Louise knew in the long term, but I would have to choose when that was.

On Wednesday morning, while I was talking to Bob in the yard, a gleaming black Range Rover, with heavily-tinted windows drove in, and parked alongside the Bentley. Two well-built men climbed out of the car, as I walked towards them. They were both casually dressed and wearing black windcheaters, partially zipped up.
'Can I help you?'
'Hi, Mr Cavendish,' said the taller man, in an American accent.
'Do I know you?'
'Nope... but we know you, sir.'
'So it seems... so, who are you and what do you want?' I asked.
'Can we go someplace and talk?' he asked.
'Not until you tell me who you are!' I persisted.
'We're from the American Embassy, sir... so, can we talk in private?'
On hearing that my spine began to tingle, before I said, 'okay, let's go into the house.'
They followed me into my study, where I waved them to sit, and asked, 'so, who are you and what's this all about?' As if I hadn't guessed!
'I'm Ralf Harwood and this is Mitch Cooper, we're special security agents, attached to the embassy,' Harwood replied.
'I see... and, how does this affect me?'
'You visited a Chinese businessman, named Mr Lu Ming, last Sunday...'

'I did… and, what's that got to do with you?' I interrupted.

'We're interested in anyone who calls on Mr Ming…'

'And, how did you find me?' I interrupted.

Cooper replied, 'we monitor our CCTV continually, and checked the number plate of your Bentley with the authorities, sir… so, it was easy.'

'Oh, really… that easy?'

'Yup.'

'Now, tell me why you're here?'

Harwood replied, 'we think you can help us…'

'To do what?' I interrupted… fearing that I was about to be asked to get involved in more murky business.

'For various security reasons, the US, at Langley, want to know what Mr Ming is involved in… and so, we need to gather as much 'Intel' as we can on him… business deals, movements in and out of the country… that sort of thing.'

'Well, I don't know how I can help you.'

'We know you were an Air Force pilot, and that you flew on missions in Afghanistan…'

'So… what's that got to do with anything?' I interrupted.

'…You may be asked to fly Lu Ming out of the country, under the radar, so to speak… we'll be monitoring your smart little Cessna, that you keep here on the farm,' replied Harwood, and I thought, *well, they've certainly done their homework!*

'I don't think that's very likely… and besides, if I did fly Lu Ming out of the country, the CAA would know, because I'd have to file a flight plan… and, I'm sure they'd be quick to inform you,' I replied, with a wry smile.

'Just so, Mr Cavendish… but, we would like to be informed before the event, and not sometime after,' Harwood countered, with a knowing smile.

'Let's be absolutely clear, sir… we're here because we want to know what Lu Ming is up to, so please co-operate, and inform us of any business deals you're made aware of, or flights he intends to take… here is my card,' Cooper said, as he produced his card and placed it on the desk.

'…And here's mine,' said Harwood, as he did the same.

'We'll leave you now, Mr Cavendish… but, rest assured we'll

be watching over you from now on… for sure,' said Cooper… and I thought anxiously, *for some reason, I don't doubt it!*

As they stood to leave, Harwood said, 'we'll show ourselves out, sir… have a nice day,' and with that they were gone. I followed them outside, just in time to see the Range Rover pull away and leave the yard. A moment later, Louise joined me, asking, 'who were those men, darling?'

'They're American agents, from the Embassy…'

'And, what did they want with you?'

'They're making inquiries about our Mr Ming.'

'Do you think he's a spy?'

'…I've no idea.'

'I'm getting more and more worried about all of this,' she said, firmly.

'So am I… but, there's nothing we can do about right now, so let's go in and have a coffee.'

Roger and Naomi arrived late on Friday night and, over drinks, offered their apologies… it appeared that Roger had been unexpectedly delayed in court, and had a mountain of paperwork to finish, before he left his chambers.

'It always seems to be the same, these days,' said Naomi, with a touch of annoyance, before she grudgingly sipped her tonic water… wishing she could have a gin.

'But my darling… it's work that I desperately need,' replied Roger, and I noticed Louise shake her head… I guessed we were in for a fractious weekend, but a lot worse was yet to come.

'So, when's the baby due?' asked Louise brightly.

'In April,' replied Naomi with a smile.

'Ah, a spring baby… how lovely,' said Louise.

'Yes… and, we're really looking forward to it.'

'As long as it's not twins!' said Roger, and we laughed, while Naomi didn't seem to appreciate the joke.

Over breakfast, the next morning, they seemed more at ease, and Roger suggested we all go for a walk around the farm… but, Naomi said she would prefer to rest, and maybe do something later… so, Roger and I set off in the morning sunshine, to tour the acres of wheat and barley. As we were alone, I thought it a good opportunity to question him about Macmillan and his acquaintances; in the hope that I could discover who, if it wasn't Lu Ming, was making enquiries about the old team… but, I didn't get a chance, as I'd just opened my mouth to speak, when he said, 'I'm so glad to be here, Peter.'

'Well, you know we're always pleased to have you and Naomi stay with us.'

'I know… thanks for that, you're a good friend.'

'Yes, you're right' I said confidently… now, I'd like to ask you about…'

'Peter, I desperately need your advice,' he interrupted.

'…About what?'

'I have a few dreadful problems.'

'…Only a few?' I joked, and he smiled.

'Yes… I think… Peter, you're the only person I can turn to' he replied. It wasn't too difficult to figure out, so I asked, 'you haven't got *more* women troubles?'

'Yes, of course I have… you know me so well!'

'Indeed, I do… unfortunately…'

'Well, for start Kate is pregnant…'

'Dear God, Roger!'

'I know… I know… I should have been more careful.'

'Does Naomi know?'

'No, of course not… but, she'll probably find out… Kate wants to have the baby, and she expects me to pay for it!'

'And, so you bloody well should!'

'But, can you imagine…? This is a lifelong, financial commitment… clothes, holidays, school fees, and God knows what else!' he said, as he stopped and stared at me; imploring me to magic a solution out of thin air.

'Well, you should have thought about that when you were busy bonking!'

'Oh, I know *that*, but I need advice now, not bloody contraception! Should I insist that she has an abortion?'

'You're an arrogant bastard at times, Roger… do you actually think you have the right?' I replied firmly.

'Peter… I really don't know what to do, for the life of me,' he whined.

'Listen to me, Roger, you have to get a grip, and stand by Naomi… you know it's the right thing to do!' I exclaimed, but he shook his head slowly… 'There's more,' he said, as he walked on, 'I'm in serious trouble with another woman, as well.'

I sighed and said, wearily, '…go on… enlighten me.'

'Before Macmillan was shot last year, I went with Anne to a drinks 'bash' of his, for foreign businessmen. These were the select few who contributed to party coffers… he introduced us to a seriously rich Chinese guy, called Lu Ming… and, I thought, 'oh no… not Leisha!' as Roger continued, 'and his gorgeous wife, Leisha.'

I thought, 'Oh dear God… what a mess!' and asked, 'so, are you having an affair with her?'

'Well, off and on… it's a bit complicated,' he replied.

'So, try me.'

'A few days after we met at the drinks party, she phoned me in chambers, and said she was out shopping in the West End, and would I like to join her for lunch…'

'And, so you did…'

'Yes, and during the meal Leisha told me that she was much younger than her husband, and that she was his third wife…' he said, then paused.

'Go on.'

'She complained that he was so busy with business and travelling, that he neglected her… and her sexual needs.'

'…No surprise there then.'

'Quite… a week later she invited me to their country house, near Witney…'

'…In Oxfordshire?'

'Yes… it's a lovely place.'

'I'm sure it is.'

'… And, her husband was away again… in Hong Kong, I think…'

'So, you kindly filled in for him, so to speak?'

'I did… but, I couldn't resist her, Peter… she is the most erotic woman I have ever met!'

'You say that about all of them, but tell me more…'

'Well, I can only see her when her husband is away, as we have to be so careful he doesn't find out.'

'…Of course.'

'Leisha totally captivates me… she is able to do things with her body, that have astounded me…would you believe that she can shoot ping pong balls from her fanny?… No wonder the Chinese are so good at table tennis!'

'Roger!'

'She's just amazing…totally amazing!'

'I'm sure that's one way to describe her… and I presume her husband is a jealous man?'

'Yes, apparently… and violent…Leisha says he has several vile, dangerous men, who do his dirty work for him,' he replied, and I felt a nervous tingle in my spine, as I managed to whisper, 'really?'

'Oh, yes… and, wouldn't you be jealous, with a gorgeous wife like Leisha, who can do such fantastic tricks?' he asked.

'Possibly,' I replied, and wondered if my good friend would end up on Lu Ming's list of the 'necessary dead'… ultimately requiring my disposal service!

During our walk, while he droned on about Leisha, I occasionally managed to ask him about Macmillan's team, and told him what Natasha had said, but he knew nothing that I didn't already. I decided not to tell him that I had met Lu Ming and his talented wife, but would wait until another time… I hoped I was doing the right thing.

CHAPTER 3

WHAT EVER NEXT, I WONDER?

Louise and I spent the rest of the weekend walking on eggshells, to ensure that Roger and Naomi remained talking to each other. There was obviously a tension between them, that you could cut with a knife... so much so, that we were relieved when they finally said 'goodbye' to us, on Sunday afternoon.

As Louise waved to their departing BMW, she said, 'well, I don't think that marriage will last much longer.'

'I'm sure you're right.'

'Marrying a mistress is usually the most stupid thing any man can do.'

'I agree, darling... thank heavens I've never had one.'

'Quite... and, make sure you never do!'

Monday and Tuesday passed quickly by, and Louise started packing for a few days away, with her mother, Julia. The plan was that they would drive down to the in-laws cottage, overlooking the sea at Perranporth, in Cornwall, and Rob and I would join them on Friday night, for a restful weekend. On the Wednesday morning, we said 'goodbye' with lots of kisses, and I waved to Louise and the babes, as my wife drove off to collect Julia, from her house, on the other side of the village.

That evening, I had just finished eating my dinner, of fish and chips, microwaved straight out of the freezer, when my phone rang.... I hoped it wasn't Lu Ming.

'Hello.'

'Hello, darling... we've arrived safely,' said Louise, and I sighed with relief.

'Oh, good, and how are the babes?'

'...Just fine.'

'And how's Julia?'

'Mum's okay. Busy tidying the place up and making beds.'

'Well, a woman's work is never done...'

'You can say that again!' Louise interrupted, I chuckled.
'So, phone me when you can.'
'Of course… and, be early when you come down on Friday.'
'We will… providing your Dad isn't late back from work,' I replied.
'Right… love you.'
'Love you too.'
'And don't do anything…'
'Like what?' I interrupted.
'Anything I wouldn't approve of!'
'…Of course not.'
'Love you…bye, darling.'
'Bye.'

Within a few minutes my phone rang again… and again, I hoped it wasn't Lu Ming… and it wasn't… but, it was his wife!
'Hello.'
'Mr Cavendish?'
'Yes, speaking, Mrs Ming,' I replied, instantly recognising Leisha's voice.
'I must see you…'
'Why?' I interrupted, fearing something awful.
'I have a terrible problem.'
'I'm not sure I can help you...'
'You must… Lu said you were a man who could be relied on,' she interrupted.
'Well, I hope I can, but…'
'My husband is in Switzerland at the moment, but I don't know exactly where … I phoned the Hotel Kempinski, in Geneva; where he said he was staying… but, they say he wasn't booked in there, and had made no reservation,' she said anxiously, as her voice began to break. A shiver ran down my spine, and a host of questions cascaded through my mind. *Had Lu Min been murdered… or maybe kidnapped?* God only knows!
In the circumstances, I relented and asked, 'so what's the problem?'
'It's my mother… no, Lu's mother… I'm so confused… she has done something awful!' Leisha replied, and I thought, 'well,

some mother-in-law's do upset the family apple cart, now and then.'

'So, what has she done, Mrs Ming?' I asked, fearing she'd left the bathroom untidy again.

'She's strangled our maid!'

'Dear God,' I whispered, and asked, 'is she dead?'

'I don't know…'

'Well, can you find out?'

'She's in the other room…'

'…Your maid?'

'No, Lu's mother…'

'Where's the maid?'

'Upstairs,' she replied, and knowing that Leisha was frightened and confused, I calmly asked, 'please go upstairs and find out if your maid is still breathing…'

'Oh please just come, Mr Cavendish!' she pleaded.

'Please listen to me…'

'I don't know what to do!' she interrupted.

'If she's still alive, call an ambulance… and, if she's dead, you have to call the police…'

'I can't do that!'

'…Why not?'

'Because they won't believe it was an accident, and they'll find out that Lu's mother is here… and, she's not supposed to be!'

'So, where is she supposed to be?'

'…In Beijing!'

'She's here illegally?'

'Yes… and, my husband would never forgive me if she's sent back to Beijing… please come and help me, Mr Cavendish… please.'

It was the second desperate 'please' that spurred me to action, and I said, 'alright, I'll come… are you at home?'

'No… I'm at our country house, near Witney.'

'What's the address?' I asked, and she gave it to me.

Within minutes, I was in the Bentley, with my mind in a whirl; speeding towards the Manor House, in the village of Minster Lovell, just outside Witney. If I managed to sort this little mess out, it would cost Lu Ming a great deal of cash... providing he was still alive, of course!

As my speedy journey progressed, I wondered if the American Agents, or their colleagues, were following me, so I kept glancing in my rear view mirror, to look for their black Range Rover. It didn't appear, and I felt quite relaxed... then it occurred to me that they were probably watching the house in Minster Lovell. If they were there, then I would be questioned intensely, just for visiting... which was not a happy prospect!

By the time I reached Minster Lovell it was dark, and I searched for the Manor House, eventually finding it at the end of a poorly-lit, leafy lane. I didn't see any other vehicles parked close by, and it was a comfort to know that I wasn't being observed. As soon as I pulled up in the driveway and stepped from the Bentley, Leisha appeared in the doorway, her slim figure silhouetted by the light of the hallway. She visibly sagged with relief, gushing 'thank you, thank you... thank you so much for coming, Mr Cavendish.'

I just nodded and said, '... where's the maid?'

'Still upstairs... I'll take you to her.'

'Is she alive?' I asked, as I followed Leisha into the house, and up the magnificent wooden staircase.

'I don't know...'

'Well, why haven't you found out yet?' I asked impatiently, as we reached the spacious landing.

'I don't know, I'm scared to find out... she's in there,' replied Leisha, pointing to a half open door. I stepped into the well-furnished bedroom, and immediately saw the young woman lying by the side of a king-sized bed. I knelt down, and searched for a pulse in her neck... there was none. I noticed she had red, brutal marks around her throat. I stood up, looked at Leisha, and said, 'I'm afraid she's dead.' She shook her head, and said in a whisper, 'I can't believe it.'

'Where's your mother-in-law now?'

'...In her room.'

'Does she realise what she's done?'

'I don't think so.'

'Well, you'd better find out.'

'I can't do that...she's too upset.'

'Would you like me to talk to her?'

'No... she doesn't speak English,' Leisha replied, and we both remained silent for a moment, gazing down at the lifeless body, as I tried to gather my thoughts.

'If you think it's not possible to call the police, for whatever reasons...what do you want me to do?'

'Just get rid of her,' Leisha replied.

'Will she be missed by anyone?'

'No... her parents are dead, and she has no other relatives in China.'

'Hmm... is anyone else in the house, who knows what's happened?'

'No, only my husband's mother is here... we're alone, Mr Cavendish.'

'I see... tell me, when do you expect your husband to return from Switzerland?'

'I'm not sure... in about a week or so... he's usually never away any longer than that,' she replied, and I nodded, thinking, *if he doesn't come back, it'll be a real mess, involving the Americans and the police, who will have some difficult questions for me!*

I looked at the body again, made a snap decision, and said, 'I'll take her... get a blanket.'

'Oh, thank you, Mr Cavendish... I'm sure you will be well rewarded by my husband,' she said, with relief, before quickly producing a blanket, from a nearby chest of drawers. I wrapped the body and lifted it easily, before carrying it down stairs and out to the car. After gently placing the body in the boot, I said, 'goodbye, Mrs Ming...ask your husband to contact me, when he arrives home.'

'I will Mr Cavendish, goodbye... and, thank you.' I nodded, slipped behind the wheel and drove off into the night. As I left the lane, I glanced at the clock on the dashboard. It was just after eleven, so, all being well, I could be back at the farm by about three... which was time enough to fly out over the Atlantic, and dispose of the maid, before Bob and the boys were about.

I arrived back home as it was just getting light, and drove down to my Cessna, parked at the top of the strip. I opened the door of

Papa Oscar, and placed the body of the lifeless maid into the passenger seat, strapped her in, and returned the Bentley to its usual parking space. Just as I stepped from the car, I heard Bob's voice behind me, saying, 'morning boss,' which took me by surprise, and set my heart racing. I turned to face him and replied anxiously, 'morning, Bob... you're up and about early this morning.'

'Yes, we've got a lot on today... so, it's best to make an early start,' he replied, with a smile.

'Yes, good thinking, Bob,' I said, hoping against hope he hadn't seen me carrying the maid.

'Are you going flying now?' he asked.

'Yes, just a short one... it's so good in still air, in the morning.'

'I'd like to come with you, if I may, boss.'

My sphincter tightened, as I replied, 'you're welcome any time, Bob, but I thought you'd got a lot on today... and, I wouldn't want to stop you.'

'Well, if it's only a short flight, I think the boys could manage without me,' he persisted, and I didn't know what to say to get to out of this situation... as I was about to make some half-hearted reply, Jim's voice called out, 'morning, boss.' I turned around to see him smiling and replied, 'morning, Jim... you're another early bird.'

'Yes, we've got to crack on today... Bob keeps us at it,' he replied.

'I'm pleased to hear it,' I said, as Paul arrived, and said, 'morning.'

Bob looked disappointed, saying, 'I was just going for a flight with the boss, but now you're both here, I'd better stay and crack the whip, or you two buggers'll be shirking!'

'No peace for the wicked,' said Jim, with a sigh, and we all smiled, before I said, 'catch you later, boys,' and walked off down to Papa Oscar. I breathed a long sigh of relief, as I untied the aircraft, checked the fuel levels in the wing tanks, and climbed aboard. I quickly carried out the cockpit checks, started the engine and opened the throttle. Within yards Papa Oscar lifted up from the strip and, I physically relaxed, as she climbed effortlessly to a thousand feet, and I headed out across Lyme Bay. I checked the time; it was nearly four o'clock, so I intended to fly for an hour, at the usual cruising speed of one hundred knots, which would take me a hundred nautical miles out to sea; where I would dispose of the unfortunate Chinese maid. I set the trim to climb gently, and when the Cessna reached two thousand feet, I re-trimmed to maintain level flight, and checked the instruments. Everything looked okay, and I settled down for the monotonous flight over the grey sea.

Suddenly the engine fluttered, but then continued to run smoothly again. I hurriedly scanned the instruments, and noted that everything seemed to be in order, when the flutter came again. I felt anxious, as engine failure over the cold sea, would mean a ditching which would be difficult to survive. I scanned the instruments once more, I had plenty of fuel, the engine temperature and oil pressures were okay... then the engine fluttered again, and began to run very roughly... before it hit me! I had neglected to pull the carburettor heat knob to the 'on' position, to stop the carburettor from icing up, which I should have done every ten minutes or so, when flying in cold, moist conditions. I prayed that I wasn't too late, as I yanked the knob into the 'full heat' position.

The engine continued to misfire, as Papa Oscar lost height, and I realised that unless the heat melted the accumulated ice in the carburettor, I would have to ditch... and, I had no life jacket with me! The aircraft slowly lost height, with a fluttering, misfiring engine, and all I could do was hope that the ice melted in time. I watched the altimeter unwind to five hundred feet, with my heart in my mouth, as I prepared to ditch into the cold, grey sea. I was about to send out a 'Mayday' message, when the engine stopped fluttering, and began to run a little more smoothly... but still occasionally uneven. I breathed a sigh of relief, and began to pull gently back on the control column, to gain some height above the cold, restless sea below.

It seemed an age before the engine ran smoothly continuously, but once the ice had completely melted, Papa Oscar climbed slowly back to a thousand feet. I re-trimmed to continue the gentle climb to two thousand feet, and when the altimeter eventually showed Papa Oscar had reached the altitude, I re-trimmed for level flight. I was still sweating, but trying to focus on the next phase of the flight, as I glanced at my watch. I had been airborne for forty minutes, so only had another twenty minutes, before I could say 'goodbye' to the maid, and return home. Every minute seemed like a lifetime, I constantly glanced at my watch, willing the time to pass. At last the moment had arrived, I undid the door latch, released the maid's seatbelt, and banked Papa Oscar over, to push her out to her watery grave. As I reached across, I was taken aback by the sight of a large container ship, below me, ploughing through the heavy sea! I was shocked and somewhat concerned that I hadn't noticed the vessel before now; realising I'd been looking at my watch, and not paying proper attention. I quickly brought the aircraft into level flight, and gently turned to head in the opposite direction of the cargo ship, in order to put as much distance as possible between us, before disposing of the body.

I flew for another ten minutes, and then banked Papa Oscar to a steep turn, pushed the maid out, and watched her plummet down to the sea, where she disappeared beneath the waves, with barely a splash. I thought *what a cruel world... God help us, and forgive us for what we do.*

I returned to the strip in a melancholy mood, and landed safely... then, as I shut down the engine, I thanked my guardian angel, for watching over me again... he (or she)... well you never know what sex they are... had been awfully busy recently.

I went into the house, made some coffee, and sat contemplating what might happen next. I really didn't have a clue, so I tried to put it to the back of my mind. That's when Mary Hill arrived, to cook breakfast. Mary was Louise's aunt, and had been Uncle Ted's housekeeper, after his wife, Aunt Jane had died.
 'Morning, Peter,' she said, brightly.
 'Morning, Mary... how're you today?'
 'Fine thanks, just fine... and, who wouldn't be on such a lovely

day?'

And I thought, *me, for one...* but replied, 'oh absolutely.'

'So, what do you fancy for breakfast?'

'I don't mind, Mary.'

'Right... I'll cook a pan of everything!' and, she did... it was delicious!

Later, I was sitting in the study, reading through the latest information from Brussels, regarding arable farming subsidies, when my phone rang.

'Hello.'

'Hi, Mr Cavendish... Mitch Cooper speaking.'

I sighed, and asked, 'so, what can I do for you today, Mr Cooper?'

'Do you happen to know where Lu Ming is at present?'

'No, I don't.'

'Are you sure, sir?'

'Positive.'

'Now, are you really sure?' he persisted.

'I am.'

'Well, we know you went to his house in Oxfordshire last night... so, would you like to think again, sir?'

My blood ran cold, before I replied, 'Mr Cooper, I don't know how you knew that I drove up to Witney last night...'

'Well, I can easily answer that, sir...'

'Oh really?'

'Sure, we have a clever network of cameras, which recognise number plates, and yours pinged up just outside Witney...'

I thought, 'dear God, they're watching every move I make!' and replied, 'well, just because I visited his house, it doesn't mean I know where he is, Mr Cooper.'

'I get that, sir, but we have to ask.'

'Of course... will that be all?'

'No, I'm afraid not... did you see his wife?'

'I did.'

'And, did she give any idea of where he was?'

I hesitated, and decided to tell him, 'yes, she told me he may be in Switzerland, but she didn't know for certain where he was.'

'Hmm... okay... we'll be in touch, Mr Cavendish.'
'I'm sure you will!'
'Have a nice day,' he said, abruptly, before he hung up.

I sat thinking for some time, and decided that whatever happened from now on, I wouldn't dispose of any more bodies. My latest experience over the sea was a nightmare, and as the Americans were closing in, I thought it was time to call a halt to my early morning activities.

I phoned Aunt Paula, just to talk, but decided that, as the Americans were probably listening to my calls, it would be safer to fly up to Kidlington and see her. Paula was pleased to hear from me, and I told her I would be with her at lunchtime.

'Then, I'll rustle up something for us to eat, Peter,' she said, with a chuckle.

'I'm sure you will Paula... I'll see you soon... Bye.'

As I flew over the green countryside, at two thousand feet, I felt quite relaxed, knowing my disposal activities were now over. I landed Papa Oscar at the busy airport, paid my landing fees, and took a taxi out to Yarnton, where my lovely aunt greeted me, with kisses and a hug... which I needed!

'So, Peter, what have you been up to?' she asked, as she led the way into her kitchen.

'Oh you wouldn't believe it,' I replied, slumping down on a chair.

Paula looked at me and said, 'that bad, uh?'

'Yup.'

'So, tell me all, while I cook,' she said... and, I did.

Paula was anxious about the American involvement, saying, 'you have to be very careful from now on, Peter.'

'I will be, and I've made the decision that I won't be flying at night over the sea, disposing of bodies any more... no matter what.'

'I'm pleased to hear it... so, what will you tell Lu Ming if he asks you to?'

'I don't know, I'll have to think,' I replied.

'Well, you'd better be ready with a good excuse, because I've been in contact with some of my business friends in Hong Kong, and they all tell me that he is well known as a sharp, ruthless character, who has no problem using violence, if he deems it necessary.'

'So his wife told me,' I said, and Paula sighed.

'Dear God, you're in deep, Peter.'

'Maybe… but not as deep as Roger.'

'Is he involved?'

'Yes… he's having an affair with Lu Ming's wife.'

'The bloody fool!'

'My feelings exactly!'

'Well, if what I'm told about this man is true, then you could soon be asked to dispose of Roger, when Lu Ming finds out about the affair… and, he will.'

'But, I thought Roger was happily married to Naomi?'

'We thought so too.'

'So, is that now on the rocks?'

'Seems so… and, to make matters worse, she's pregnant… and, so is Kate, his bit on the side!'

'Dear God Almighty… some men are foolish in the extreme!'

'I agree, Paula.'

'So, what is so attractive about this Lu Ming's wife?'

'She is very beautiful, much younger than Ming; she's his third wife… and apparently she can do sex tricks,' I replied.

'Well, Roger does like that sort of thing.'

'Indeed, it seems he does…'

'… So, what does she do that fascinates him so?'

I drew in a deep breath, and replied, 'she can shoot ping pong balls from her fanny.' Paula looked stunned for a moment, then burst out laughing, saying, 'well you couldn't make it up!'

'Possibly not,' I said, and joined in the laughter.

She had tears in her eyes, as she said, with a giggle, 'please don't tell me anymore… I'll never be able to finish cooking lunch.'

'I won't, I promise.'

We hardly spoke during the delicious lunch, which consisted of a mushroom omelette, followed by soft ice cream, covered in chocolate. Over coffee, in Paula's drawing room, we talked for some time, and she outlined every dangerous possibility that could possibly present itself. My aunt was so incisive, yet positive about my predicament, and it made me really appreciate this truly remarkable woman. I knew I could rely on her every step of the way, as I attempted to struggle out from this dangerous swamp of murder and intrigue.

Paula drove me to Kidlington Airport, and with kisses and hugs, we said 'goodbye,' before I made my way to Papa Oscar, which was parked in the line of visiting aircraft. I checked everything, then started her up, and called the tower for departure instructions. The flight back to the farm, in the afternoon sun, was smooth and serene, and I enjoyed every moment of it... but, my peace of mind was soon to be shattered!

It was just before nine o'clock that night, when Roger phoned.
'Hello.'
'Hello Peter, it's Roger,' he said breathlessly.
'You sound a bit agitated, dear boy.'
'I bloody well am, Peter... I need your help,' he replied, and my heart sank... a friend in need is always a bloody nuisance!
'So, what's wrong?'
'I can't talk on the phone... can you come and meet me?'
'If I must, but it's getting late... '
'I know, but my life depends on it, Peter,' he interrupted, I sighed inwardly, and asked,
'Okay...where?'
'Can you get up to Oxford?'
'Oxford?'
'Yes...'
'What the hell are you doing there?' I asked, but could obviously answer my own question!
'I'm staying at the Randolph Hotel... it's in Beaumont Street... please come as quickly as you can.'
'Okay, but it'll take me quite a while to get there.'
'That's not important, as long as you come... besides, it won't take you long in that Bentley!' he said. Which made me think, *it*

would be much quicker to fly up to Kidlington, and that would mean the Americans couldn't follow me.

'Change of plan, Roger...'

'Oh dear God!' he interrupted, in fear.

'I'll fly up, and take a taxi from the airport, so I'll be with you sooner, rather than later!'

'Oh Peter, you're a good pal.'

'I know... and, don't you ever forget it!'

'I won't... see you soon.'

'I'll be there... bye.'

CHAPTER 4

WILL IT NEVER END?

It was dark by the time I landed at Kidlington, and I took a taxi to the Randolph Hotel. I went straight to reception, and called Roger, on the internal phone. He sounded relieved that I'd arrived, and I hurried up to his room, which was on the second floor. He opened the door just as I emerged from the lift, and said anxiously, 'thank God you're here, Peter.'

'Well, it's been a bit of a last minute, hasty jaunt, so it'd better be important,' I said, with a grin, as he stood back for me to enter.

'Oh God, it certainly is!' he replied, closing the door, and then asking, 'a drink?'

'No thanks,' I replied, before sitting in a chair by the window.

'Well, I need one.'

'So, what's this all about?'

'I'm in serious danger…'

'Not from another woman… I hope!' I interrupted.

'No…but, let me tell you the whole bloody story.'

I sighed, and said, 'well, I'm listening.'

He sat on the bed, took a sip of scotch, and said, 'I had a call from Leisha this afternoon, when I was at home… she sounded very upset, something to do with her mother-in-law… couldn't make head or tail of it,' he paused, and took another sip… at that moment my spine tingled, and a whole host of questions cascaded through my mind.

'Go on then.'

'Well, she desperately wanted to see me, so I drove up to Witney…'

'Does Naomi know about any of this?' I interrupted.

'No… she's gone to stay with her sister for a few days.'

'That's convenient.'

'Yes, thank God…'

'So, why are you here at the Randolph?'

'I needed a good drink to steady my nerves…and, I thought I'd be safer staying here for the night, rather than driving back to

London.'

'Hmm…an unusually good decision, for you.'

Roger nodded, took another sip of scotch, and said, 'Leisha's husband is presently away in Switzerland, so I took the opportunity to see her, and try and help if I could.'

'You're her knight in shining armour!'

He grinned, and replied, 'yes, I always like to think so.'

'Then tell me about this serious, life-threatening danger you're in.'

'When I left her house this evening, I saw a black Range Rover parked at the end of the lane…' on hearing that my spine began to really tingle, as he continued, 'I thought it strange, but ignored it… then I noticed it was following me through Witney.'

'So, what did you do?'

'When I got to the roundabout on the A40, I went around it three times, just to see if I was really being followed…'

'… And were you?'

'Oh yes, the Range Rover stuck so close I thought the bloody thing was going to hit me!'

'Then what happened?'

'Once we were on the A40, heading towards Oxford, I put my foot down, but still couldn't shake it off… '

'Dear God,' I whispered.

'Then on a fast stretch it overtook me, pulled in front, and slammed on its brakes… well, I can tell you, that really scared me, but worse was to come…'

'Go on.'

'I nearly hit the back of it, but managed to stop just in time… then, these two blokes got out… built like proverbial brick houses, they were… they came back to my car as I wound down my window, and said, 'can I help you?'

'So, what happened then?' I asked, knowing that the Americans were obviously behind this little drama, but Roger surprised me with his reply…

'I could see by their little slitty eyes that they were Chinese…'

'Chinese?'

'Oh yes… mad bastards… and they kept asking me where Lu Ming was… I said, I didn't know, but they didn't believe me…

45

and, I think they were about to drag me out of my car when a police car pulled up behind me...'

'... And obviously that saved you!'

'Yes... and, when the buggers saw the police, they scurried back to their Range Rover and drove off, at speed!'

'You've had a lucky escape then.'

'Without a doubt... the policeman asked if everything was okay, and then told me I shouldn't have stopped on a dual carriageway anyway... there's always something with the police, isn't there?'

'Yes... always... so, did you tell him about the Chinese?'

'No... I thought it might cause some trouble, that's why I called you...'

I sighed, shook my head, and said, 'Roger, what the hell do you think I can do to help you?'

'I don't know, but you'll think of something to get these Chinese buggers off my back... you always do,' he replied.

'Well, if you'll take my advice...'

'Oh I will, dear boy, I certainly will,' he interrupted, enthusiastically.

'Then for a start, I advise you to stop seeing Leisha, otherwise...'

'I can't possibly do that!' he interrupted, in alarm.

'Why ever not?'

'Well, for one thing, she's the most wonderful woman I've ever met...'

'But Roger, you said that about Naomi, Kate and Nicole...'

'I know, but I hadn't met Leisha then, had I?'

'Roger... you're a lost cause, because you're someone who will never, ever learn... you are completely beyond any help!'

'Peter...'

'...And, when Lu Ming finds out about your affair, he'll cut your bollocks off... and then, probably chop the rest of you into little pieces... before all your body parts are shipped back to China, to be buried somewhere in the mountains, beyond the Great Wall!'

On hearing that, Roger's jaw dropped with shock, his eyes widened, and he was unable to speak, as I continued, 'so, you have a choice... give her up, or face a dreadful, painful death!'

'Oh my God!' he whispered. I believed that the only way to stop my friend from descending into the dark abyss of this disaster, which was entirely of his own making, was to shock him. And it worked, or so I thought... but future events would prove otherwise!

'So, I'll leave you to think about it, Roger...'

'Don't go... for God's sake, don't leave me!'

'I must... I'm going down to Cornwall tomorrow, to be with Louise, the babes and her parents, for a quiet weekend.'

'... So, you're leaving me here to face these Chinese killers?'

'Roger, if you really think your life is in danger, then call the police!'

'I can't possibly do that.'

'Why not?'

'Because it will be on police records, and I just can't have that... not with my position at the Bar to consider,' he replied.

'Roger... you seem to have all your priorities in life the wrong way around... that's why I think you're beyond any help!'

'But Peter...'

'Goodnight, Roger... call me after you've thought about what I've said,' I interrupted, before leaving the room, making my way out of the hotel, and hailing a taxi, to take me to Yarnton. I phoned Paula, on the way, to tell her I needed to see her, urgently.

Paula greeted me with smiles, kisses and a hug, saying, 'well, this is an unexpected pleasure.'

'Yes, I know... but, I need your advice, Paula.'

'... Well, it's always nice to be needed, if only for advice,' she said, with a smile, before leading me through into the drawing room.

'Drink?' she asked, as I slumped down on the settee.

'No, thanks... I've flown up, and need to keep a clear head.'

'You've flown up just to see me?' she asked, with a mischievous smile.

'No... actually, it was because of a desperate call from Roger.'

'Oh really,' she said, in an unimpressed tone, and then continued, 'more women trouble, no doubt!'

'Well partly…'

'I guessed as much,' she interrupted.

'He had a phone call from Leisha this afternoon, and went to Witney to see her, because…'

'…Her husband is away and she needed some relief!' interrupted Paula, with a grin.

'Not quite… but, after he'd seen to her, he left, and was followed by a Range Rover; which forced him to stop on the A40…'

'Now, this does sound exciting!'

'I thought it was our American friends, but two Chinese got out and asked him where Lu Ming was, he said he didn't know, and just as they were about to drag him from his car, a police car pulled up… and, the Chinese scurried back to their Range Rover and drove away at speed.'

'Well, it's seems he had a lucky escape, this time!'

'Quite so…'

'And, what did the police want?'

'Just to check he was okay, and told him he shouldn't stop on a dual carriageway.'

'That's typical.'

'… And, he phoned from the Randolph, and begged me to see him… he sounded desperate, so I flew up.'

'… So, what did he want?'

'My help…'

'Again?'

'Yes… and, after he told me what had happened, I told him to give Leisha up… or when Lu Ming finds out about their affair, he'll cut Roger's bollocks off, and then chop the rest of him into little bits, before shipping his body parts back to China, for burial in the mountains.'

'At the very least!'

'But, he said he could never give her up, so I told him he was beyond any help.'

'Sounds as if he is, Peter, but you've done your best.'

'Have I really?'

'Yes, you have, darling.'

'I don't think so, Paula… that's why I've come to you for

advice.'

'Hmm… I'll have to think about this, because I'm not sure I've any answers for a foolish man, in serious trouble, that he's brought upon himself… and, won't listen to his best friend.'

I sighed and said, 'I know just how you feel, but you know better than anyone how to persuade a man…'

'Oh, if only!' she said, with a scoff, raising her eyebrows.

'Now, don't be shy about your powers…'

'I'm never shy!'

'I've noticed,' I replied, with a chuckle.

Paula sat in silence for a few moments, and then said, 'do you know… I think he'll leave Naomi, and go off with this Leisha…'

'Oh, dear God, no... surely not.'

'Surely yes!'

'What makes you think that?'

'Because I've seen men hopelessly attracted to such women, and it always ends in complete disaster,' she replied.

'Then, that is precisely why I must help Roger get out of this mess!'

Paula sighed, 'You're right… and, we'll think of something.'

'Thanks… I knew I could rely on you.'

'Well, it's the least I can do for my favourite nephew,' she said, with a chuckle.

We talked for some time, and made plans, before Paula drove me to Kidlington. After kisses, we said 'goodbye,' promising to keep in touch. The flight back home was serene, in bright moonlight; calming and so enjoyable. As the lights from the civilisations below intermittently passed beneath my wings, followed by the countryside, bathed in a pale silvery shimmering glow, I felt at peace… which, obviously, was not to last!

I arrived over the strip and made a low level pass, just to check everything was clear for a landing, and to my horror, spotted some cows in the middle of the runway. I cursed and made a low approach, and switched on the landing light, in the hope that I'd frighten them away. I lined Papa Oscar up with the runway; selected five degrees of flap, to give me lift, and gave full throttle to the engine, as I flew over the grazing cattle. I banked the aircraft steeply, and looked back at the strip, in the middle of the climbing turn... but to my surprise, my low-level escapade hadn't frightened the bloody cows away... they remained, calmly, chewing the grass!

I thought *this is all I need!* Before I flew another circuit, and lined Papa Oscar up with the runway once again... determined to put abject fear into the cattle, which had obviously strayed from the adjacent farm. I flew lower and faster on this approach, and gunned the engine when I was right over the cows. As I climbed out and turned, I looked back and saw that they had scattered... all but one! Have you noticed, that in any given situation, there's always one? I thought about diverting to the club at West Compton, and landing there, but knew that could be tricky with a hard runway, and no landing lights on... I could end up damaging the undercarriage. I climbed Papa Oscar up to five hundred feet, and thought about the alternatives... what would I do if I couldn't shift the bloody cow? I would certainly have words with Jason Brett, the neighbouring dairy farmer, at the earliest opportunity!

I could always divert to Bournemouth Airport, or stay airborne until it got light enough to land at West Compton... so, I checked my watch and the fuel levels, in both tanks. It was just before one o'clock, and I had enough fuel for at least two hours flying, on cruise throttle settings.

I decided to stay airborne, after I had one more try to shift the contended cow; which was still busily chewing up my grass strip! I was determined... I dived down to a dangerously low level, and gunned the engine, as I swished over the cow, then turned my speed into height, before looking back in the climbing turn... it was still there... now, with its back to me!

I thought, 'it's time to give up!' and climbed to five hundred feet, set the throttle to cruise and trimmed out for a wide circuit, above the farm. As I gazed at the moonlit scene below me, I suddenly noticed lights coming from outside the barn, where I'd parked the Bentley. I watched the lights intently, and saw them move... I realised it was our farm Land Rover, driving down to the strip, with either Bob or one of the boys at the wheel... and, knew I was saved.

I watched the Land Rover with relief, as it made its way to where the cow was still munching; the driver almost had to ram into it, before the stubborn animal finally moved off. After the cow had departed, the Land Rover drove back to the top of the strip, the driver got out, and silhouetted in the headlights, started waving at me with both arms. I turned Papa Oscar towards the driver, lowered the nose, then flashed my landing light off and on, which made him wave back frantically. I waggled the wings to acknowledge, and set the aircraft up for a final approach. I selected five degrees of flap, throttled back, allowed the speed to decay, then rounded out, and touched down safely, on the strip. As I taxied up to the house, I could see that the driver was Bob... bless him! After I'd shut down and climbed out of the cockpit, he came towards me, and said, with a smile, 'I heard the plane go over twice, and guessed you were in trouble, boss.'

'Yes, I was...'

'Brett's cows are often straying into our fields.'

'Then it's high time I had a serious word with him, Bob.'

'Good... his cowman takes no notice of me, when I tell him!'

'Well, I'll put that right... and, thanks for coming out to save me, from having to fly around until it got light,' I smiled.

'It's no problem, boss.'

I thanked him once again, before going into the house and making some much-needed coffee. As I sat at the kitchen table, sipping the sweet reviver, and thinking about all the events of the night, I came to the conclusion that I should now tell Louise everything. Paula was right, my wife needed to know all about my dangerous activities... I just hoped she would understand, and forgive me.

I rested for most of the day, and just attended to some paperwork, until Rob phoned to say he was now home from work, where he's a senior customs officer, in Weymouth: he was ready to drive down to Cornwall. After I had collected him in the Bentley and we were just leaving the village, he asked in a serious tone, 'so, what the devil are you up to, Peter?'

My blood ran cold for a moment, as worrying thoughts came to mind, before I replied, 'I don't know what you mean, Rob.'

'...These flights of yours, in the dead of night... the whole village is talking about them, you know.'

'Really?'

'Yes... last night, you must have woken up half the county, going around and around, revving your engine...'

'Well, a bloody herd of Brett's cows had strayed onto my strip... I couldn't land, and I was trying to scare them off!' I interrupted impatiently, hoping that would stop Rob from asking any more difficult questions... but, it didn't!

'But, it seems, you are often flying off in the middle of the night, and everyone is now asking awkward questions.'

'Like who for instance?'

'Most people I speak to in the village pub... and, Julia daren't go into the Post Office, for fear of having to answer questions about you,' he replied, then continued, 'and the gossip rumour mill is working at full tilt... you wouldn't believe some of the stories!'

'Oh, yes, I probably would!'

'So, tell me... what are you really up to?'

I didn't know what to say, so remained quiet for a few moments, as I struggled to think of a plausible answer.

'Well?' he persisted.

'Last night, I got a phone call from Roger... he was staying at the Randolph Hotel, in Oxford... he said he was in trouble and needed my help, so I flew up to Kidlington, to try and sort things out...'

'Women problems no doubt?' he interrupted.

'Yes... what else?'

'Then, he's a fool...'

'Yes he is, but he's my friend, so I have to try and help.'

'Hmm... well, I suppose you must, but that was last night... so, what about all the other times?'

'They were early morning flights, Rob... when the air was still, and I needed to fly for some peace and relaxation.'

'Really?'

'Yes, really... and, after flying many low-level operations in Afghanistan, where some ugly bearded Taliban, perched on a hill with a rocket launcher, could really spoil your day, I can tell you that you really do need to unwind from the possibility of instant death!'

'Yes, I can sympathise with that, Peter.'

'...And, you need get a sense of perspective in life... everyone has to have someplace to recover... mine is up in the air, in the mornings.'

'Well, yes, I can understand that, I suppose,' he said, grudgingly.

'...So, you can tell all the village gossips that I'm much better now, after marrying Louise, and having the babes... so, my morning flights are soon likely to be a thing of the past.'

'That's good, because I can tell you that you're being watched...'

'Who by?'

'I don't know, but I've had a whisper from on high at work, that you are under some kind of surveillance.... So, your flying off in the mornings has obviously raised concerns.'

'I've just told you that I'll stop soon... but, only when I'm ready.'

'Good... I'll say no more and leave you to keep to it, for the sake of Louise and the twins.'

'Thank you, Rob,' I said, while wondering what the Americans were telling the authorities.

Rob said no more about my flights during the journey down to Cornwall, which was a relief... it gave me time to think. We all had a wonderfully relaxing weekend in Perranporth, and it was only when I was driving Louise and the babes home that it came up again. Rob and Julia were following on in Louise's car, and I expect were talking about me and my late night flights, while Louise was sitting in back of the Bentley with the babes, in their car seats.

'Dad said you flew up to Oxford to see Roger on Thursday night ...'

'Yes, I did.'

'So, what was that all about?' she asked.

'Need you ask?'

'More women trouble I guess.'
'You're right as usual, darling.'
'So, tell me all.'
'He said he'd had a call, from Leisha…'
'The Chinese woman?'
'Yes…so, he went to her home in Witney…'
'… And, I suppose her husband was away?'
'Of course…'
'Where?'
'In Switzerland…'
'Then, what happened…?'
'He was followed from her house, and forced to stop on the A40, by two Chinese thugs, who demanded to know where Lu Ming was… Roger told them he didn't know, and just as they were just about to drag him out of his BMW, a police car pulled up, and they scrambled back to their car and drove off,' I replied.

'Dear God Almighty…
'Quite.'
'So, what did he expect you to do about it all?'
'He just wanted to talk…'
'… And you flew up just to talk?'
'I did… he was very frightened…'
'… And, according to Dad, so were half the village, with you flying around and around, disturbing everyone!'
'I'm sorry about that, but Brett's damn cows were on the strip, and I was trying to frighten them off.'
'Hmm.'
'Darling, when we get home I'll tell you everything… and, I mean everything,' I said in a convincing tone.
'Well, I knew there was more to come,' she said.
'Yes, I'm sure you did.'
'… And, I just hope it's not as bad as my fears, because I'm really worried about you, and what you're mixed up in.'
'I promise you, darling, that everything is fine…'
'I wish I could believe that!' she interrupted.
'You can,' I replied, and we didn't talk about it again.

As we were tired when we got home, I planned to tell Louise

everything the next morning, after breakfast… but, then Roger phoned just after eight when we were in the kitchen, and it all went out of the window!

'Have you seen the news this morning, Peter?'

'No, Roger, we've only just got up… you know we've been down in Perranporth for the weekend, and arrived home late last night.'

'Well, it's all over the television… some bloody Chinaman has been found… shot dead, in a car, parked in a layby near Witney!' he said anxiously.

I whispered, 'dear God,' and asked, 'do they know who he is?' wondering if it was Lu Ming.

'No… I haven't heard anything… do you think it's one of the buggers who stopped me?'

'How the hell would I know, Roger?'

'We have to meet to discuss this, before the police start asking me awkward questions…'

'… And why should they do that?' I interrupted.

'Because the copper, who came to my rescue on Thursday night is bound to have reported it!' and on hearing that, I knew he was right… we had to meet!

CHAPTER 5

THE DEAD ORIENTAL

I went to the drawing room and switched on the television, while Louise attended to the babes in the kitchen… without asking any questions about Roger's call…I knew that would come later!
The screen had an earnest looking BBC reporter talking to camera, with blue and white police tape stretched out behind him.

'…The body was discovered last night by a passing motorist, who called the police, here at Witney in Oxfordshire… according to an eye witness, the man appears to be Chinese, although that cannot be verified at the moment… and, it seems he was shot in the head, through the side window of the car, which is parked in the layby behind me.' At that point the reporter turned away from camera and gestured towards a car, partially covered by a white tent.
He turned back, and continued, 'and, as you can see, forensic officers are examining the vehicle before it is removed… there will be a press briefing later this morning, when we will learn more about this incident… now, it's back to you in the studio.'

I waited to see if there was any further information from the news presenter, but she changed the bulletin to overseas aid, and I switched off.

I phoned Roger and said, 'I've just seen it on the news…'

'We have to meet before the police come after me!' he interrupted, anxiously.

'Okay… when and where?'

'As soon as possible… at my club… we can chat over coffee, and get things straight…'

'They'll never be straight with you, Roger.'

'Well, you're bloody wrong about that, dear boy, because since our meeting at the Randolph, I've given a lot of thought about what you said, and I've decided to give Leisha up… her old, vicious husband can have her all to himself, as far as I'm concerned.'

'I'm glad to hear it… at least your bollocks will be safe!'

'Don't be flippant… just get to my club as quick as you can, you know where it is.'

'Yes I do, but it's impossible for me to get up to London this morning…I'm in Dorset remember!'

'Well, I can't come all the way down there… I'm in court this afternoon!'

'Then let's meet half way… I'll fly up to White Waltham, which is a small airfield near Maidenhead… so, make your way there, and I'll meet you in the clubhouse.'

'Oh, alright…if you insist,' he said, with a sigh.

'It's the only way, if we're going to meet today, Roger.'

'Okay… and, before I set off, I'll have a few quiet words with my police commissioner friend, and see if I can find out more about this dead Chinese bloke.'

'That would be helpful, Roger… I'll be with you soon.'

'Good man.'

I'd just put the phone down, when Louise appeared in the doorway, and asked, 'well?'

'That was Roger…'

'I already knew that!' she interrupted angrily.

I sighed and said, 'he wants to see me about a Chinaman, who's been found shot dead, near Lu Ming's home, in Witney.'

'Hmm… oh really?

'Yes.'

'So, does he think the police will suspect him?'

'Probably… so, I'll fly up to White Waltham and meet him there, so we can talk.'

'Why can't you talk on the phone?'

'Because the Americans are probably listening in and…'

'God Almighty… what are you involved in now?' she interrupted.

'It's complicated, but I'll explain…'

'You said that last night, Peter!'

'I know, but…'

Louise shook her head in despair, sighed and said, 'don't bother!' and returned to the kitchen. I knew that time was now running out, for my explanation of what I'd been involved in, over the last year… and, my wife was not going to stand for much more. I would have to tell her everything soon, or face the possibility of a rift between us, that would never heal. Women need to know everything about a man; otherwise a sudden departure is more than likely!

After saying 'goodbye' to Louise and kissing her long face, and then the babes, I went out to find Bob. I told him I would be away for most of the day, before I checked out Papa Oscar for the flight.

The flight was smooth, and I enjoyed the low-level approach to White Waltham, from the west… which is necessary to keep below the passenger departures from Heathrow, and clear of the London Terminal Area. I radioed the tower and was given joining instructions, and then I joined the circuit and landed Papa Oscar, before taxiing to the park for visiting aircraft. After paying the landing fees, I went off to find Roger. He was already in the club house, and his face lit up when he saw me.

'Glad to see you, Peter… I thought that you might be delayed for some reason, and we wouldn't get a chance to talk.'

'Well, here I am… let's have some coffee first.'

'Yes of course, but I think it's a bit too public in here, to talk,' he half whispered.

'Then, we'll go out and sit in Papa Oscar.'

'Good thinking.'

Over coffee, I asked after Naomi, and he said she was 'okay', but didn't sound too convinced. Then, we chatted about nothing in particular, before we went out and climbed aboard my aircraft. Roger cleared his throat, and said, 'I'm sure I'm being watched…'

'… And, what makes you think that?' I interrupted.

'Wherever I drive, I see cars following me…'

'You're probably imagining it, after your brush with the Chinese, on the A40!'

'Don't think so.'

'Talking about Chinese… did you find out anything from your police friend about the one who was shot dead?'

'Well, he couldn't be absolutely sure, but said the word is that he is connected with the Chinese Embassy, in Portland Place,' he replied… which sent a shiver down my spine. Was this Oriental shot by Lu Ming, before he could kill him?

'… And how does your friend know this?'

'The car he was in is on permanent hire to the embassy,' he replied. On hearing that, I knew that Lu Ming was probably right about the Chinese Government's plan to assassinate him… so, who shot the assassin, waiting in the layby? Was it Lu Ming's thugs, or Lu Ming himself? I supposed I would find out in due course, and could see Roger was pale-faced and obviously frightened, which he confirmed when he said, 'you know, Peter, I must get away somewhere until this all blows over.'

'Hmm… I agree,' I replied, and thought, 'it would be very convenient to get Roger away for a while, so that the link with Leisha might really wither… and, it would give me some time to plan, without having to worry about him.'

'So, where do you suggest I go?' he asked.

'To our villa, in the South of France!'

He looked surprised, and replied, 'well, I supposed it is worth thinking about…but, I thought that was Paula's place?'

'She provided the finance, but it's ours.'

'Well, you lucky old thing you!'

'Oh yes… now you could fly from Luton to Marseille in under two hours, take a taxi out to the villa in Cassis, and relax by the pool for a couple of weeks… and, you'd be completely safe, because no one would know you were there.'

'It's bloody tempting, but I don't think Naomi would come.'

'Of course, she would… '

'You don't know her like I do!' he interrupted, with a sigh.

'Well, if she refuses, let me talk to her.'

'You'd be wasting your time… we're not on the best of terms at the moment.'

'I gathered that… but, Louise may be able to coax her into spending some time away, by the pool, in the sun…'

'Not with me!'

'Roger, I despair of you…'

'Why?'

'You're a well-educated, intelligent man, with absolutely no bloody common sense!'

He was taken aback for a moment, so I continued, 'you have the chance to take a break, in France, away from all your problems, and you constantly raise objections!'

'Do I?'

'Yes you do... now, go back home and tell Naomi that you've planned a little holiday for her, and if you can't persuade her, call me... and, by the way, get another mobile phone, because if what you say about being followed is true, your calls may be being listened to...'

He looked shocked, and asked, 'is that a possibility?'

'Of course... so, do as I say and take a break,' and I made a mental note to change my own phone.

He nodded, and replied, 'I'll try... if circumstances permit...'

'Here you go again!' I interrupted, and he smiled, saying, 'okay, okay... I'll go.'

'Good... let me know when, I'll let the agent, Madame Dalmas, know you're coming... she has a set of keys, and will arrange everything for you.'

'Thanks, Peter... you are a good mate.'

We said our 'goodbyes,' and he climbed out, and made his way back to the car park, while I checked everything and started up, before calling the tower for immediate departure.

As I flew back to the farm, I thought about what I would say to Louise, which now concerned me greatly. Was now the right time to tell her everything? I was still undecided, so put it to the back of my mind, for the time being... I know, I know... I should tell her, but wanted to leave it until Roger and Naomi were away.

Louise was in the kitchen with the babes, and she looked up as I walked in, and asked, 'well?'

I sighed, sat at the table, and replied, 'he's very frightened, so I've suggested that he gets away for a while.'

'Hmm... where?'

'I said he and Naomi could take a break at our villa...'

'What?' she interrupted angrily.

'I thought it best...'

'Oh really?' she interrupted.

'Yes...'

'Well, you could have asked me first!'

'I had to make a decision, darling, because...'

'Don't bother to tell me anymore,' she said, with a sigh, and I realised that the time had now come.

I looked at Louise, smiled and said, 'after dinner tonight, when the babes are in bed, we'll just sit and talk about it all.' My lovely wife smiled, and whispered, 'okay.'

We sat in the drawing room and had several large scotches, before I began to tell Louise the whole, dreadful story. I left nothing out, although I did gloss over my experience with nymphomaniac Natasha, in her pleasure room. My wife sat quietly, while I went into great detail, and laughed when I told her about Mrs Lovensky falling over in the mud, as she tried to help me lift Papa Oscar from the pothole, in France.

When I had eventually finished, she asked in a serious tone, 'did you ever hurt anyone, darling?'

'No, never... I only disposed of the bodies,' I replied, and she nodded, before taking a long, slow sip of scotch.

'... And, you ended up in this nightmare, all because of bloody Roger!'

I whispered, 'yes,' with a nod.

'Well, I've never really liked him... he's a bit too slippery for my liking.'

'I'm sorry to hear that, darling.'

'... And, if he's such good friend of yours, then how on earth would he allow you to get caught up in all this?'

'Because he's weak,' I replied.

'Particularly when it comes to women!'

'That's true.'

'...And why didn't you tell me all this before?'

I sighed, and replied, 'because I thought you'd be so shocked that you would leave me... and I didn't want to put you in an awkward position... you were a serving police officer, at the time.'

'I am bloody shocked, but I'd never leave you,' Louise replied, and at that moment my phone rang... I hoped it wasn't Roger...

and, it wasn't…. it was Lu Ming!

'Hello.'

'Good evening, Mr Cavendish… I hope you're well.'

'Yes I am, thank you, Mr Ming,' I replied, glancing at Louise, who raised her eyes and whispered, 'dear God.'

'I'm pleased to hear it,' smarmed the Oriental.

'I presume you're back from Switzerland?'

'Yes… I arrived in London this afternoon… now, my wife has told me all about your help with our delicate matter.'

'I always help when I can, Mr Ming.'

'Of course you do… and, you must be rewarded for your troubles.'

'What have you in mind?' I asked, hoping it was fifty thousand pounds.

'Can you come to my house, in London, tomorrow afternoon?'

'Possibly.'

'Please make it certain, Mr Cavendish… I want to reward you and discuss another matter… shall we say three o'clock?'

'We will.'

'Good… bye, Mr Cavendish.'

'Bye.'

I tossed the phone down, and looked at Louise, who asked, 'well, what was that all about?'

'He wants to see me in London tomorrow afternoon.'

'…And, are you going?'

'Of course… he wants to reward me for my help.'

'Hmm… well, I hope he hasn't any other plans for you.'

'We'll have to see, won't we?'

'Darling, please don't get involved with this man again… he's real trouble!'

'Let's see what he wants first.'

'… And, this time make sure you tell me everything!'

'I will… I promise.'

Next morning I set off in the Bentley, and drove steadily up to London. I planned to leave the car in the Marble Arch underground car park, and take a taxi to Grosvenor Square, because I didn't want to appear on the embassy CCTV. I didn't wish to excite our American friends any further, and have to answer any more of their damned questions again.

I arrived at the car park just before two, parked near the Hyde Park exit and, as it was a fine day, decided to walk to Grosvenor Square. I glanced at my watch as I entered the square, it was ten to three, so I made my way to number forty two, and rang the bell. The door was opened by a new, sweet little Chinese maid, who said, 'ah, Mr Cavendish, nice to see you, sir... please come in, the master is expecting you.'

'Thank you.'

'Please wait here, while I tell him you've arrived.'

'Thank you.'

She disappeared through the double doors, and quickly emerged, saying, 'this way, sir.'

I nodded, walked into Lu Ming's study, as he stood up from his desk.

'Ah, Mr Cavendish, I'm so glad that you've come this afternoon... please be seated,' he said, as he waved me to sit. I smiled and sat, as he spoke to the maid in Cantonese... she nodded and left the study.

'Now, Mr Cavendish... firstly, I must thank you for helping my dear wife, and for disposing of the unfortunate maid, who caused such problems at our country home.'

'I was pleased to help your wife, when she was in such a difficult situation...'

'...And, it is very much appreciated by us both, I can assure you,' he interrupted, and I thought, 'so, where's my reward?' as he continued, 'and as I promised, you must have a proper payment, so please accept fifty thousand pounds, in cash.'

He bent down behind his desk, and produced a black briefcase, placed it on the top and clicked open the catches, to reveal neat bundles of notes.

'Thank you, Mr Ming... you're a man of your word,' I said with a smile, and he shrugged slightly, replying, 'of course, I am,' as he closed the case.

'You said that you had another matter to discuss with me?'

'Yes...I need you to fly me out of the country, to a small airfield near the French border with Switzerland,' he replied.

'Where and when, Mr Ming?'

'The airfield is near the town of Besancon, and I want to fly out in three days... that's next Wednesday,' he replied.

'I see...'

'Can you do it, Mr Cavendish?' he interrupted anxiously, and I guessed that something was troubling him... could it be the something to do with the person, who was shot in the embassy car?

'Yes of course it's possible... but, I'll need the more details about the airfield... is it a grass strip or tarmac? Length of runway and surrounding high ground, as it must be near the Alps.'

'Very well, I'll make enquiries, and let you know.'

'Thank you... and, I suggest you write everything in a short note, and send it to me by courier.'

'Why?'

'Because I believe my phone, and possibly yours, is being tapped,' I replied, and he gave me an inscrutable smile, replying, 'you don't have to worry, Mr Cavendish... I have friends in high places.'

'... And does that include the American Embassy?' I asked... he looked anxious, as he asked, 'what do you know about the Americans?'

'Not a lot, I'm afraid, but they visited me at my farm, and asked a lot of questions about you,' I replied, thinking that after giving me fifty thousand in cash, I owed it to him.

We discussed the visit to the farm by Harwood and Cooper, which obviously concerned Lu Ming, before I asked if he had any connection with the murder of the Chinaman, shot near his home in Witney.

'No... I was shocked when I heard it on the news,' he replied, but I was sure he wasn't telling me the truth.

'But surely you must have suspected that you were a target for an assassin?'

'...Possibly.'

'You told me when we first met that your Government wanted you dead, Mr Ming.... now, just tell me about the man who was found shot in the layby.'

He hesitated before replying, 'I think that one of my staff may have done it to protect me.'

'Well, don't you know?'

'No... not for sure... the man had left for China before I arrived home, Mr Cavendish.'

'So, it remains a mystery.'

'Yes, unfortunately.

'But, you must think you are in imminent danger now?'

'Yes, I do.'

'...And is that why you want me to fly you to the Swiss border?'

'No, not at all... I'm conducting some important business in Zürich, and I wish to arrive unseen by the authorities,' he replied, with a smile.

'I see... and, will Mrs Ming be going with you?'

'No, it's just me, Mr Cavendish.'

'Right... please let me have the details of the airfield, as soon as possible, so I may plan the flight.'

'I will... and, I want to fly out on Wednesday morning.'

'Very well... so, where do you want me to collect you?'

'I'll be staying at the Randolph Hotel, in Oxford, on Tuesday night... so, collect me from there at ten o'clock, Mr Cavendish.'

'Yes, of course... and, the flight payment will be?'

'Considerable, Mr Cavendish, because you'll have to wait at the airfield until I return from Zürich,' he said with a smile, which concerned me.

'...And, how long do you expect to be in Zürich?'

'Only a day or so, then we can return,' he replied, and I nodded, thinking that Louise would not be happy about that arrangement.

After assuring him that everything would be as he instructed, we said our 'goodbyes,' and I left the house, with the briefcase, containing fifty thousand pounds. Walking back to the car park, I began to formulate my ideas, to overcome the Aviation Authorities' requirements, for flight plans across France. By the time I arrived home, I had a clear idea of how I would deceive the authorities... and, it gave me quite a thrill.

Louise was not happy about the proposed trip to France, but softened slightly when I showed her the money… with more to come, when I returned from France. After dinner, I went to my study, sorted out my aviation maps of France, and planned the flight to Besancon. It lay just over three hundred nautical miles from Calais; my flight would take me north of Paris, and the waypoint was Reims. Cruising at one hundred knots, the journey time would be just over three hours from Calais. I planned to fly to up to Kidlington and refuel there, before collecting Lu Ming, from The Randolph. With full tanks, Papa Oscar had a flight duration of five hours on cruise, which would enable me to reach Besancon safely, with fuel to spare.

After plotting my course across France, I phoned Paula, and told her I would call and see her on Wednesday morning. She was pleased about that, and said we could have a long chat over coffee, but I had other ideas, and would tell her face to face. This was a ploy to fool anyone listening to my conversation, who would think it was a meeting arranged between lovers.

The next two days passed quickly, and I was becoming anxious, as I had not yet received the airfield details from Lu Ming. The courier arrived on Tuesday evening, which was a relief, and I quickly glanced down the details; I was pleased to note that it was a small flying club near Besancon, with grass runways and the major strip ran on a heading of two-two-zero to the south west: the general direction of prevailing winds. There was no high ground in the vicinity of the airfield, which was another plus. The main runway was three hundred metres long, which was more than enough for me to land Papa Oscar safely, with ten degrees of flap. So, after a final, careful check over my aircraft, everything was now set for the flight the next day, and I went to bed excited by the prospect of the flight.

CHAPTER 6

A FLIGHT TO REMEMBER

After kissing Louise and the babes 'goodbye' at the kitchen table, I grabbed my overnight bag, containing the necessities for a short stay, and left the house. The air was clear and crisp, as I climbed aboard Papa Oscar and started up. I called Phil on the radio at West Compton, for departure clearance, and told him I was flying up to Kidlington; then possibly onto Le Touquet, and if that was the case I would file a flight plan in mid-air, after departing from Kidlington.

'Right... well, have a nice time, Peter.'

'I will.'

'... And, bring back a bottle or two for me, if you decide to nip across the Channel!'

'You can be sure,' I replied, as I opened the throttle and began the ground-run, before lifting the Cessna off the grass into the still air. The flight up to Kidlington was smooth and enjoyable. After re-fuelling, and paying the landing fee, I took a taxi out to Yarnton where Paula, wearing only her flimsy dressing gown, which showed her fulsome figure, greeted me with a hugs and a big kiss at the door.

'I didn't expect you this early, Peter,' she said, as she led the way into the kitchen.

'... And, that's for a reason, Paula.'

'Oh, do tell,' she said as she clicked the kettle on.

'I want you to drive me to the Randolph, in Oxford, to collect Lu Ming.'

She turned around, open mouthed with surprise, before asking, 'what the devil are you up to now?'

'I'm flying him over to France... in secret,' I replied, with a smile.

'My God... you're a glutton for dangerous punishment!'

'So it seems.'

'...And, why do you want me to drive you into Oxford... can't you take a taxi?'

'That's the point... firstly, I don't want any loud-mouthed taxi driver telling anybody about me collecting Lu Ming, especially the police... and, secondly, I want you to meet him.'

'Why on earth do you...?'

'Because you're my insurance, if anything goes wrong!' I interrupted.

'...And could it?'

'You never know, Paula,' I replied, she shook her head, and said, 'well, you'd better tell me all about this trip of yours.'

I glanced at my watch, it was just before nine o'clock, and I said, 'you'd better get dressed, Paula, we're expected at the hotel by ten, so I'll tell you in the car.'

'Rush, rush, rush... dear God, I thought that had all stopped after I sold the business!'

Paula drove her BMW at speed to Oxford, while I told her everything about Lu Ming and my flight to France, before we reached the hotel, just on time. She waited at the entrance while I went in search of Lu Ming, who was sitting in the reception. After polite greetings, I led him out to the car and, when he was seated in the back, I introduced him to Paula.

'Mr Ming, this is my Aunt Paula,' I said, as Paula turned round to face him.

'How do you do,' he said politely... but, I could see by his expression, he was not happy.

'Pleased to meet you, Mr Ming,' she replied, with a smile, before she started the car and we drove off. During the journey, we remained silent, and only when we drove into the airport, stopping by the control tower, did Paula say, 'we're here now... so, have a safe trip.'

'Thanks, Paula,' I replied.

After she had driven off in the BMW, Ming said, 'your aunt is a very attractive woman.'

'Indeed she is.'

'Is she married, Mr Cavendish?'

'Not anymore!'

'Hmm,' he mused, with a smile, before we walked along to the parking area for visiting aircraft, and climbed aboard Papa Oscar.

After I had carried out all the cockpit checks, and we were wearing our headphones, I asked Lu Ming if he was ready to go.

'Yes, Mr Cavendish, I am... and, how long will it take us to get there?'

'We're about an hour's flight from Le Touquet...'

'Le Touquet?' he interrupted in alarm.

'Yes, I plan to land there as part of my plan to confuse French Air Traffic of our final destination,' I replied.

'... And, how do you propose to do that, Mr Cavendish?'

'By telling them I'm going for a local area flight, to enjoy the scenery... and, will possibly land at a convenient airfield and stay the night.'

'Won't they be suspicious?'

'No, because so many French pilots do that all the time, and their Air Traffic Control are quite relaxed about the whole touring thing... they're not as fussy as our CAA,' I replied, as I started the engine.

I called for clearance from the tower, informing them I was returning to my farm strip in Dorset. Once I received go-ahead, I taxied out to the runway threshold, where I checked magnetos, engine temperatures and pressures. The tower gave me clearance to depart, so I entered the runway, opened the throttle, and within yards the Cessna lifted off into the air.

As we climbed to a thousand feet, Ming asked, 'and how long will it take to get to Besancon, from Le Touquet?'

'About three hours... we'll be cruising at a hundred knots,' I replied.

'That's good to know,' he replied, as I set a course towards the farm strip. After about ten minutes, I called Kidlington tower and told them I was changing radio frequency to West Compton. Having done that, along with the customary thanks, I called Phil and told him I was now flying to Le Touquet, and I filed a mid-air flight plan. Everything was now set for the flight to Besancon, via Le Touquet, and I felt quite elated at the prospect.

I flew along the coast to the Dover VOR (navigational beacon), called Air Traffic Control, and relayed flight details, before heading out across the Channel, while glancing down at the ferries below; who were busy dodging the stream of container ships.

Midway across, I called the French Air Traffic at Calais, informing them I was inbound to Le Touquet, and I was given clearance. The town of Boulogne passed slowly under my left wing, and then Le Touquet came into view. After calling the tower, I followed instructions and landed, before parking Papa Oscar. After paying the landing fee, in the control tower, I told the officer that I would be leaving soon for a local area flight, and would probably land somewhere near Reims, and stay the night. He smiled and wished me a good trip. I had left Lu Ming in the café, adjacent to the control tower, and I joined him for a coffee and croissant, before we strode out to Papa Oscar, to begin our flight to Besancon.

After a smooth take-off, I climbed the Cessna to a thousand feet, and set the course for Reims. The airspeed soon built up to one hundred knots in level flight, with the correct throttle settings for cruise. The French countryside passed gently under the wings, as I checked the compass heading, while occasionally glancing at my map, in order to verify various features and landmarks. All was well; we were on course and would soon reach the way-point of Reims.

I told Lu Ming, but he didn't seem very impressed… in fact, he looked concerned, if not positively anxious. I asked him if all was well, and he told me that flying was not his favourite mode of transport… especially in small aircraft! I ignored the comment, wondering why on earth he had asked me to fly him to Besancon, but guessed it must be for a good reason… and, somehow connected to his nefarious business, in Switzerland. As long as I was to be well paid for the trip, I didn't really care much.

In a short while, Reims came into sight, with its glorious cathedral, and I checked my watch… we were within minutes of my calculated arrival time, and as we approached, I called Reims control… informing them that we were on a local area flight, out of Le Touquet. With local flight information and pleasantries exchanged, I ended the radio call, but listened out for conflicting traffic in the area.

Soon after leaving Reims, the glittering Swiss Alps came into view, through the afternoon haze, and I knew that we would soon arrive at Besancon. I called the flying club, on the radio frequency I had from my details in the European flight manual, and informed the tower that we were inbound, and should arrive within half an hour. Lu Ming looked pleased after he heard me say that; he visibly relaxed and smiled.

'Not long now until we land, and soon you'll be in Switzerland,' I said, and he nodded.

'Good, Mr Cavendish.'

'... And how long do you expect to be?'

'I should return to Besancon by tomorrow afternoon... so, you won't have to wait too long,' he replied. So, all being well, I'd only have to stay one night, somewhere near the club, and I was sure that someone would recommend a local hotel. I put all thoughts out of mind and concentrated on finding the airfield, which came into view at my ten o'clock, so I gently banked Papa Oscar around, to begin my approach. I called the tower and received joining instructions for a left hand circuit, for a landing on runway two two zero.

With five degrees of flap, I lowered Papa Oscar down onto the runway, taxied to the turnoff and made my way around to the control tower, then shut down the engine and all systems.

'So, we're here, sir.'

'Yes... thank you, Mr Cavendish.'

'Have you a car waiting for you?'

'Yes... I have,' he replied, as he undid his seat belt, and opened the door.

With a quick nod of his head, he turned and said, 'goodbye, I'll see you tomorrow afternoon, Mr Cavendish.'

'Goodbye, sir.'

Lu Ming walked away briskly towards a large, black Mercedes with tinted windows, which was parked near the tower. A chauffeur stepped out and opened the rear door for him, and he climbed into the dark interior. Within moments, the Mercedes had disappeared from view, and I made my way up to the tower, to pay the landing fee.

'We do not have many English pilots landing here,' said the controller, with a smile, as I handed him my credit card.

'No, I don't expect you do.'

'So, monsieur, are you staying long?'

'…Just until tomorrow.'

'Then are you touring around France?'

'No, I don't think so.'

'Ah, back to England then,' he said, with a smile.

'Yes, probably… now, tell me, do you have overnight accommodation, here at the club?'

'No, unfortunately not, monsieur, but there is a small hotel called, 'Le Moulin Bleu,' quite close by… it's on the road to Besancon.'

'Thanks.'

'… And you can order a taxi in the club room; the barman has the number, monsieur.'

'You've been very helpful,' I replied with a smile, as he handed back my card, and was just about to leave, when he asked, 'and the gentleman, who arrived with you… will he be going back to England?' I thought this question a little too inquisitive for my liking, but replied, 'yes… he will be.'

'Ah, bon… here on business, I expect.'

'Possibly…why do you ask?'

'We just like to check on any arrival of strangers… it's the Gendarmerie who insist, monsieur,' he replied, with a smile.

'Yes, of course,' I replied, before walking out of the office. As I made my way to the clubhouse, I felt slightly concerned about the Gendarmerie making any inquiries.

Outside the clubhouse were people sitting at tables, under large sun umbrellas, chatting and drinking; most of them stopped and stared at me, as I approached. Some smiled, as I gave them a nod, while others looked a little hostile, as if I was invading their private club. Inside the clubhouse, a few people were at the bar drinking, and they turned to look at me with suspicion, but a very attractive young woman smiled. I returned the smile and was enchanted by her lovely looks. She was petite, with her lustrous black hair cut in a long bob, her brown eyes and perfect complexion enhanced her beautiful face. I asked the barman for the taxi phone number, but he pretended he didn't understand me, and replied in French. The lovely woman said in English, with a smile, 'it's over there on the notice board, monsieur.'

'Thank you, mademoiselle,' I replied, and she blushed a little.

I made my way over to the board, and as I looked for the number amongst all the other information, I was aware of the petite woman standing next to me.

'Where do you wish to go, monsieur?' she asked.

'Ah, the hotel, 'Le Moulin Bleu'… it's on the road to Besancon…'

'Oui, I know where it is, monsieur,' she interrupted, with a smile.

'I'm sure you do.'

'Let me drive you there…'

'Oh, I wouldn't want to trouble you, mademoiselle,' I interrupted.

'It's no trouble, monsieur… I live there…'

'You live there?'

'Oui, my parents own it… so, shall we go?' she asked, with a smile… I was speechless, and just nodded.

'Do you have some luggage?'

'Yes, it's in my aircraft,' I replied.

'Bon, I'll come with you, monsieur.'

After collecting my overnight bag and locking Papa Oscar, she led me to the small car park where her little blue Renault was parked. When we were sat inside, I said, 'this is very kind of you, mademoiselle….'

'My name is Hélène Dubois, but please call me Hélène,' she interrupted, as she started the engine, asking, 'and what is your name, monsieur?'

'Peter… Peter Cavendish.'

'Ah, Pierre… my favourite name!' she exclaimed, before we roared out of the car park at speed, while I hung on for dear life.

As we hurried along the road to Besancon, she asked, 'have you been flying long, Pierre?'

'Yes… I was a pilot in the Air Force for twelve years, flying fast jets…'

'Mon Dieu!' she interrupted.

'Then I retired, and now just fly for pleasure.'

'I have my licence also… and, love to fly in the Alps.'

'Really… I think that's a bit dangerous.'

'I like a little danger… it is always so exciting… don't you think?'

'Possibly,' I replied with a smile, as I knew this petite lovely was being very suggestive, so I would have to watch out.

'So, why don't you let me fly you round the mountains?'

'That would be good, if I had the time, but I'm only here overnight.'

'Oh, shame, but you could come over from England again and stay.'

'I could, and next time I would bring my wife and children,' I replied, and watched her face drop a little.

'Oui, that would be nice,' she said without conviction, as the Renault slowed then turned into the drive leading up to Le Moulin Bleu hotel.

I followed Hélène into the lobby of the small hotel, where a woman at reception looked up and spoke to Hélène in French.
Hélène replied in English, 'Mama, this is Monsieur Cavendish, who's just arrived from England, and needs a room for tonight.'

'Ah, welcome, Monsieur Cavendish,' said Mama, with a smile.

'Thank you, madam.'

After booking in, Hélène showed me to my room, and said, 'I'll see you later, Pierre,' before she hurried away, leaving me speechless. The room was comfortably furnished with a small en-suite, but as I was only there for the night, it would be adequate. I sat on the bed and tried to call Louise, but the signal was hopeless, so I thought I would try again outside, after dinner.

The dining room was full of guests, all talking loudly, as the French always do during a meal. I was shown to a small table for two, in the corner, by an attentive waiter. The menu was quite limited, so I ordered a starter of Garlic mushrooms, followed by chicken salad. The meal was delicious, and I was about to order coffee when Hélène arrived, and asked, 'may I sit with you, Pierre?'

'Yes of course,' I replied, with a smile.

'Merci... was the meal to your liking?' she asked, as she sat opposite.

'Yes, it was very good, thank you.'

'Bon... I'll tell Mama.'

'Yes, please do.'

'So, tell me all about flying jets, Pierre,' she said, with a smile. There is nothing so bewitching to a pilot than being asked by a beautiful, attentive woman with 'come to bed eyes' to 'bang on' about his flying... it is the dream of every pilot. So I obliged, and Hélène gasped with admiration in all the right places... and, I knew I was being set up for later.

After trying to call Louise from outside the hotel, without success, I returned to my room and tried the landline... eventually getting through. Our conversation was short, and I promised to be back at home by tomorrow evening. We said our 'goodbyes,' with kisses, and I had just put the phone down when there was a knock at my door. I knew who it would be... and, I was right. Hélène stood there in a floral dressing gown, holding up a bottle of wine in her right hand, and twiddling two glasses in her left.

'I thought you should have a drink to relax you after all your flying today, Pierre.'

'I don't think that's a good idea, Hélène.'

'Why?' she asked, before pushing passed me into my room, and placing the wine and glasses on the bedside table.

'Because I'm married, with two small children,' I replied.

'... And, does that stop you drinking wine, Pierre?'

'No it doesn't, but it's what comes afterwards...' I replied.

'So, what comes after?'

'You know very well!'

'Do you mean this?' she asked as she undid her dressing gown and let it fall to the floor, revealing her beautiful naked body.

'Yes, I do!'

'So, Pierre, do you like what you see?'

'Very much, but I must say 'no' to your invitation.'

'Why?'

'Because it's not right… and, I have to think of my wife.'

'But, no-one will ever know… and, I thought your last night in France should be fun!'

'I'll know!'

'Pierre, you English… how you say, *are so uptight* about love…'

'This isn't love, it's pure sex!' I interrupted.

'… And, what's wrong with that?'

'Nothing… if you like that sort of thing… but, I don't!'

Hélène looked extremely angry, and said, 'huh!'… she picked up her dressing gown, flung it over her arm, and flounced out of my room naked, saying, 'and you can take the fucking wine home to your wife!'

'Thanks,' I replied, as she slammed the door behind her, and I thought, 'hell hath no fury like a woman scorned'… but, I would be away from Hélène's fury by tomorrow afternoon.

I slept well, and after a shower, followed by a breakfast of croissants and coffee, I paid my bill and said 'goodbye' to Hélène's mother, who looked a little perplexed. I guessed her daughter had told her all about the stiff upper lipped Englishman, and she didn't approve.

A taxi took me to the airfield, where I checked Papa Oscar over for the return flight, and then re-fuelled the tanks to maximum. After that, I waited in the aircraft, with both doors open to let in the cool mountain air, breezing in from the Alps, for Lu Ming to arrive in the afternoon. I was checking my maps and the reciprocal headings, when out of the corner of my eye, I noticed someone walking towards Papa Oscar. It was Hélène, carrying a shopping bag, which she held up and then smiled.

'Bonjour, Pierre,' she said, as she arrived at the open passenger door.

'Bonjour.'

'You said you were not leaving until this afternoon, so I thought you might like some lunch.'

'Well, that's very kind.'

'I've brought cheese, baguettes and some sparkly water.'

'Thanks.'

'… And, wine for your wife… I want to say sorry for last night…'

'Please don't think any more of it.'

'So, do you forgive me?'

I replied with a smile, 'there's nothing to forgive, Hélène.'

'Oh, Pierre, you are so kind… and, I think your wife is very lucky to have you.'

'I'll tell her that when we're drinking the wine!' I said, and she laughed.

'So, may I sit in with you?'

'Of course.'

After she had climbed up and was sitting comfortably, she asked, 'so, what are you waiting for?'

'…My passenger.'

'…A woman?'

'…No, a business man, who's been driven across into Switzerland.'

'… And, when will he be back?'

'Sometime late this afternoon,' I replied, but something in my mind suddenly queried that arrangement, and I began to think for a moment.

'Hélène, if he is delayed overnight, could you book me back in your hotel?'

'Bien sûr!' she replied, with a smile.

'Thanks… '

'… And, I will come and collect you when you call… so, write my number down.'

I nodded, and she gave me the number, before I said, 'it probably won't be necessary, but you never know.'

'Of course, Pierre, but I hope I will see you again before you leave.'

We then spent a very pleasant time, talking about flying in the

Alps, and Hélène obviously had a lot of experience amongst the mountains, flying in a club Robin DR 400. We shared the baguettes and laughed a lot, before she said, 'I must go now... so, au revoir, Pierre... I hope I'll see you again.'

'I'm sure you will,' I replied, as she leaned over and gave me a little kiss on my cheek. I watched her until she disappeared into the car park, and settled back to wait for Lu Ming... but he didn't arrive!

CHAPTER 7

AN UNEXPECTED SITUATION

As the time passed, I wondered what might have delayed Lu Ming, but gave up, as it could be a myriad of things, in his dangerous, chaotic life. I occasionally glanced at the time, as I relaxed and watched the club aircraft taking off and flying towards the mountains, with a touch of envy.

It was just before seven o'clock, when I thought I should phone Hélène and ask her to book me into the hotel. She sounded delighted, and said she would come right away to collect me.

I locked up Papa Oscar, reported to the tower that I would be staying another day, and advised them if my passenger arrived, then I could be found at the hotel. I made my way to the car park as Hélène arrived, and she smiled when she saw me. She was delighted that I was staying overnight, and we chatted all the way to 'Le Moulin Bleu,' where her mother booked me in again, with an approving smile.

I went to my room, and phoned Louise on the landline to tell her I had been unexpectedly delayed, which did not please her at all. Anyway, I made my peace and we finished our conversation with kisses, before I went down to the dining room for dinner, where Hélène joined me at my table, looking stunning in a black cocktail dress.

'So, Pierre, is it okay if we have dinner together?'

'Of course,' I replied, as I waved her to sit.

Over the delicious meal, Hélène enchanted me with amusing stories, about herself and the locals, which at times, made me laugh out loud. As she drank more wine, she became funnier, and I was aware of other diners looking at me… but, I really didn't care! This young woman was a delight, and I revelled in her company. After we'd leisurely finished our coffee, she said, 'well, Pierre… I will have to go now and help Mama with the bookings, so bonne nuit.'

'Bonne nuit, Hélène.'

'... And, I will not trouble you again, like last night!'
'I'm relieved!' I replied, and she giggled.
'But, I'd like to see you fly off tomorrow.'
'Then please do, I expect my passenger in the afternoon... so, join me for lunch with some baguettes,' I replied, and she nodded before walking away, a little unsteadily.

True to her word, Hélène didn't disturb me, and I didn't see her until just before one o'clock the next day, at the airfield. She joined me in Papa Oscar with the baguettes, and we continued our conversation while we ate. As the afternoon passed, I became more concerned about Lu Ming, and asked Hélène to book me in again, if he didn't arrive.

'What do you think has happened to him, Pierre?'
'I've no idea, but I think he's probably been held up in business meetings.'
'Umm... well, I hope I'll see you tonight... then we can have dinner together.'
'That would be nice.'
'But, phone me if he arrives, as I'd liked to say "au revoir", before you fly off.'
'I promise,' I replied, with a smile, as she gave me a kiss on my cheek, and left.

Lu Ming didn't arrive, so I gave Hélène a call, and she came to fetch me from the airfield.

We were enjoying our main course in the dining room, when Hélène's Mama came in, looked about, and made her way over to our table.

I looked up at her, as she said anxiously, 'Monsieur Cavendish... there is a Gendarme in the office, and he wants to speak to you.'

'Do you know what it's about?'
'Non, Monsieur... but, you must come.'
'Of course,' I replied, fearing the worst.

Madam led the way, and Hélène followed me into the office, behind reception. There, behind a desk, sat an elegant man, who I presumed was Hélène's father, and a tall Gendarme was waiting nearby.

'Are you Peter Cavendish, monsieur?' he asked, in English.

'I am, officer.'

'Bon... we have a report from the Swiss Police that a Chinese businessman, named Lu Ming, has been involved in a serious car accident, and is in hospital...'

'Oh dear God.'

'... And, he has asked for you to visit him, as soon as you can, monsieur.'

'Of course... where is he, officer?'

The Gendarme looked at his notebook, and replied, 'he has been admitted to the Berne University Hospital, monsieur.'

'I know that hospital, my friend Monique was taken there after a skiing accident,' said Hélène brightly.

'Is it too much to ask you to drive me there, Hélène?' I asked.

'Non... of course not!'

'Then, take my car... yours is too small for a long journey... and, be careful!' said her father.

'Merci, Papa.'

The Gendarme looked serious, as he said, 'and Monsieur Cavendish, please report to the Gendarmerie, before you fly back to England.'

'Why, officer?' I asked anxiously.

'...Because Chief Bosenquet wants to talk to you.'

'...What about, officer?'

'I don't know, monsieur... but, just make sure you come and see him before you leave!' he replied emphatically, as he gave me a firm nod.

'Yes of course, officer.'

'Merci... bonne nuit,' he said, before leaving the office.

Hélène's father looked at her, and said, 'well, after you've introduced me to Monsieur Cavendish... you'd better get going.'

'Oui, Papa.... Pierre, this is my Papa... Frederic.'

'I'm pleased to meet you, monsieur,' I said, as he stood and we shook hands.

'... And, I you, monsieur.'

'Thank you for your help...'

'You must thank Hélène, she's driving you to the hospital,' he interrupted, with a knowing smile... so, I guessed I was in for a fast ride... and, I wasn't wrong!

Hélène led me out to a gleaming black BMW 5 series, and as we sat in the comfy seats and strapped in, I asked, 'how long will, it take?'
'About three hours,' she replied, and I glanced at my watch... it was just before eight, so we would be there by about eleven. Hélène engaged drive in the automatic box, and then stepped on the throttle. The big car leapt forward out of the hotel car park, and proceeded along the road at some speed, as she said, 'I love driving Papa's car... it's so fast!'
'Indeed it is, but just make sure we arrive at the hospital in one piece!' and she laughed.

Hélène drove the BMW with skill, and I was impressed with her driving ability, and was sure she was an excellent pilot. In my experience women make superb pilots, as they instinctively know how to treat an aircraft... which is sensitively and gently, and that is replicated in the controlled flight.

We hardly spoke during the journey, which was a blessing, as it left me to ponder on what would happen next. *If Lu Ming was fit enough to travel, would he want to fly back with me? If he had to stay in hospital, should I wait or go back home, until he had recovered?* And I didn't like the prospect of reporting to the Gendarmerie in Besancon, to be questioned by Chief Bosenquet, whoever he was. Everything was a mess, and there were many unanswered questions cascading through my mind, as we reached the Swiss border, and then roared along the road towards Berne. I occasionally glanced at my lovely, petite driver, as she drove the big car with consummate ease, and smiled with enjoyment.

I glanced at my watch when we arrived at the entrance to the A & E... it was ten thirty, so Hélène had made swift progress. After making enquiries at reception, we were directed up to ward 10, in the white, pristine building. A helpful ward sister told us that Lu Ming was not seriously injured, and showed us into an opulent side room, where he was sitting up in bed, with his arm in plaster. He looked relieved to see me, and said, 'ah, Cavendish... you've come at last.'

'Yes...how are you feeling?'

'Alright... I suppose... and who's that?' he asked impatiently, with a nod towards Hélène.

'Hélène Dubois... she drove me here.'

'Well, I need to talk to you alone, Cavendish.'

'I'll wait outside, Pierre,' whispered Hélène, before she discreetly disappeared.

I pulled up a chair, sat at his bedside, and he said firmly, 'it wasn't an accident... someone tried to kill me!'

'Are you sure?'

'Of course, I'm sure... I saw this black four by four, as it pulled alongside, then rammed my Mercedes...'

'Good God!' I interrupted.

'... And, he tried three times, before the bastard pushed us over the crash barrier and down into the ravine...'

'Do the police know?'

'No... they think my chauffeur was at fault, but now he's dead, so they won't be able to question him!'

'Your chauffeur was killed?' I asked, in a shocked tone.

'Yes, he was pronounced dead at the scene... and, I only survived because I was strapped in, and sitting in the back.'

'Then, you've had a lucky escape, sir.'

'I realise that, Cavendish... and, now you must get me back to England as soon as you can!'

'So, what do the doctors say about your injuries...'

'Never mind them... I plan to leave here tomorrow morning... so, you and your driver stay somewhere close tonight, then come and pick me up at ten o'clock.'

'Very good... we'll be here, sir,' I replied, and he nodded.

'Now, go... and let me rest, Cavendish.'

'Goodnight, sir.'

'Goodnight,' he murmured, as he closed his eyes.

I found Hélène in the corridor, and told her that we had to leave, so we thanked the ward sister, and did just that. In the descending lift, I told Hélène what Lu Ming had said, and she looked shocked.

'Mon Dieu, Pierre!'

'…And we have to stay here overnight, and then drive him back to the airfield, before anything else happens to him.'

'…Of course.'

'We'll try to book in at the nearest hotel, and hope they can fit us in, this late.'

'I must call Papa and let him know,' she said, as we reached the ground floor.

'Okay… and, I'll call my wife, and tell her what's happened.'

We hurried out to the BMW, and stood by the car as we made our calls, without a problem. Louise was not best pleased, but I assured I'd be back home by tomorrow night. She didn't sound convinced!

Hélène drove only a short distance, before we found the Hotel Metropole, Berne, and luckily the receptionist had two adjoining single rooms, which suited me perfectly… but, Hélène looked disappointed. We made our way up to the rooms, and Hélène suggested we raided the mini bar, in her room, for a nightcap… I told her she was wasting her time trying to get me to sleep with her, but agreed to have just one drink. I hoped I wouldn't regret it! After pouring a small scotch for each of us, she sat on the bed, and asked, 'so, Pierre, tell me about this businessman,' which made me feel a little uncomfortable… but, I decided to tell her the truth, and keep some of the more unpleasant, morbid facts from her.

'Lu Ming is a wealthy Chinaman, who contacted me through a friend…'

'A woman?' she interrupted.

'Yes…'

'Hmm… I thought so!' she said, but I ignored the comment and continued…

'… And, he asked me to fly him to various places… to which, I agreed…'

'For plenty of money!' she interrupted, while rubbing her fingers together and smiling.

'Who's telling this story?' I asked, with a grin.

'Why, you are, Pierre,' she replied, with a chuckle.

'Right... now, Lu Ming has obviously upset the powers-that-be in China, and he believes that they are going to try and kill him...'

'Mon Dieu!'

'Quite... and this latest incident, if factual, proves he was telling the truth.'

'So, you must protect him, Pierre.'

'I will if I can... but, the best thing is for me to fly him back to England, as soon as I can.'

'Of course, but I'll be sad to see you go... promise you'll come back and stay... then we can go flying in the Alps.'

'Yes, I'd like that, Hélène.'

'... And, you can bring your wife... she can stay in the hotel and talk to Mama!'

I laughed and replied, 'you've got everything planned haven't you?'

'Of course,' she said, before she finished her scotch, adding, 'I'll think I'll have another one... and you?'

'Better not, I'm flying tomorrow.'

We sat and talked for some time, about her life and flying in the mountains, until I eventually got up, gave her a quick kiss on her cheek and left the room.

After a good night's sleep, I showered, called for Hélène, and we went down to breakfast. I glanced at my watch over our coffee and croissants, and noted it was just after nine.

'We'll have to get going, if we're to book out of here and be at the hospital by ten.'

'I'm ready, Pierre... so, you just say when,' she replied, and I nodded.

I paid the bill with my plastic, while Hélène went out to the car.

Within minutes, we pulled up outside the hospital and made our way straight up to ward 10, where there had been a change of the overnight staff, so I didn't recognise the ward sister.

I smiled, and said, 'good morning, we've come to collect Mr Lu Ming.'

'... And who are you, monsieur?'

'My name's Cavendish… I'm working for Mr Ming.'
'Oh… I'm sorry, didn't you know?' she asked.
'Know what?'
'He's been arrested by the Federal Police this morning, and taken to…'
'Oh bloody hell!' I interrupted, with shock.
'… And, it must be something serious for the Federal Police to be involved…'
'Where have they taken him?' I asked, as my mind was now full of questions, and I felt that I was caught in a web, from which it would be difficult to escape.
'I am not sure, but the Gendarmerie will know,' she replied.
'Thank you,' I said, and grabbed Hélène's arm, and then headed for the lift.

Once outside the hospital, I said, 'so, let's try and find the nearest Gendarmerie.'
'Bien sûr,' she replied, before slipping behind the wheel.
We were driving towards the centre of the city, looking for some sign of the Gendarmerie, when I noticed a police car parked by the side of the road. Hélène stopped and I leapt out. I approached the officers and found that they didn't understand English well, but after I said 'Gendarmerie' several times they realised that I needed directions. They quickly drew a map of its location, I thanked them and hurried back to the BMW.

Hélène parked the car outside the impressive building; we climbed the steps, entered and made our way to reception. I asked the duty officer where Lu Ming was, and if I could see him. The officer told me to wait, and disappeared through a door behind the desk… soon after, he re-appeared with a tall man in a suit, who said, 'please come with me, monsieur.' We followed him along a nearby corridor, and into a large office at the end.
'Please sit down, monsieur and mademoiselle,' he said, as he gestured towards seats in front of his glass-topped desk.
'Thank you,' I replied, but began to feel uneasy.
'Who are you, monsieur?'
'I'm Peter Cavendish…'

'And you, mademoiselle?' he interrupted.

'...Hélène Dubois... and I'm French!'

'So, what connection do you both have with Monsieur Lu Ming?' he asked firmly.

'I am working for him,' I replied.

'... And you, mademoiselle?'

'I don't know him, and have never met him... I just drove Pierre here from Besancon.'

'Hmm... I see.'

'... And who are you, sir?' I asked impatiently.

'I'm Captain Ruedeli... and I'm in charge of special criminal investigations, monsieur.'

'So, where is Lu Ming?'

'He has been taken to Kantonspolizi Headquarters, in Zürich, for further questioning,' he replied, and my heart sank... this had turned into a game of three-dimensional chess!

'...About what?'

'I'm not at liberty to tell you, monsieur, but I must ask you some questions... and, if I am satisfied with your answers, you may leave.'

'May leave?'

'...Oui.'

'And if not, I presume you will arrest me!'

'I will monsieur... because you are a person of interest.'

'...My God!'

'So, you are obviously English... do have any identification?'

'Yes, my passport and my pilot's licence.'

'Let me see them,' he replied, and held out his hand.

I produced them from my wallet and handed them over. As he glanced through my passport, he asked, 'so why are you here, monsieur?'

'I told you... I'm working for Lu Ming.'

'I understand that you flew him to Besancon in a small, private plane... why was that?'

'Lu Ming is afraid of flying in commercial aircraft as they are open to terrorist attack,' I replied, and he looked concerned.

'Do you know of a planned terrorist attack, monsieur?'

'No, I don't... but, I would certainly inform the authorities, if I did.'

'Very public spirited of you, monsieur,' he said, with a touch of sarcasm.

'Well, I was a squadron leader, flying in the Royal Air Force, so I am loyal to my Queen and country,' I replied with a smile, which made him think.

'Hmm...'

'...And Lu Ming has been injured in a road accident, and for some obscure reason, which you are reluctant to tell me, you have taken him from the hospital, where he was receiving treatment for his injuries!' I interrupted his thoughts.

'I know that, monsieur, but my orders came directly from our headquarters in Zürich,' he replied.

'That may be so, Captain, but you must agree that refusing to tell me anything is totally unreasonable!'

He nodded slightly, and replied, 'I suggest you go to Zürich and make inquiries, monsieur.'

A few moments of stony silence followed, as we both glared at each other, before I replied, 'we will... good day, Captain.'

'Good day, monsieur... mademoiselle.'

Once outside the Gendarmerie I said to Hélène, 'are you okay to drive me to Zürich?'

'Of course, Pierre,' she replied, with a smile.

'Then let's go.'

Hélène drove quickly, and we only stopped once for fuel and a coffee, at Luzern, before arriving in Zürich.

'I suppose we'll have to stay the night,' she said with a contented smile, as we drove slowly towards the centre of the city.

'Yes... I think that's for certain.'

'Then, we'll have to find a good, comfortable hotel.'

'Of course.'

'So will your wife be angry?'

'...Probably.'

'Oh dear... and is that because you will have to spend another night with me, Pierre?'

'Louise doesn't know about you, Hélène.'

'...Mon Dieu... if only she knew!'

'Quite... now, let's try and find the police headquarters, then perhaps we can soon leave with Lu Ming.'

'Pierre, I think we'll be here for a few days yet,' she replied, with a smile... and, I was worried about that possibility myself.

We eventually found the headquarters of the Kantonspolizi, and we parked outside, before hurrying into the ornate interior. At reception, I gave our names and asked to see an officer who was dealing with Lu Ming. We were then was asked to wait, by the efficient female at the desk.

Within minutes, a well-dressed man appeared from a side door, and asked, 'Monsieur Cavendish... Mademoiselle Dubois? I am Sergeant Amstutz... please come with me.'

He led us down a long corridor to an office, and ushered us in to where a distinguished-looking man, in uniform, sat behind a large desk.

'Ah, Monsieur Cavendish... and Mademoiselle Dubois, please be seated,' he said, as he gestured to us.

'Thank you.'

'I'm Captain Boschert... and, I'm in charge of investigating criminal financial activity,' he said, and my heart sank. This was likely to take some time, until Lu Ming was released... if ever!

'... And may I know the charges against my employer, Lu Ming?' I asked, as the sergeant sat to one side of Boschert, and began to take notes.

'In time, monsieur... you say that you are his employee?'

'That is so, Captain.'

'Then, you will be able to answer the many questions that surround Lu Ming's activities...'

My mind reeled, as I realised how little I knew about his trip to Zürich, other than it was on business... so, I replied, 'Captain, I know nothing about his business activities.'

'...But, you said you were working for him, monsieur... so, surely you know something?'

'Well, no... I just flew him here...'

'So I've been informed.... And, I must ask why in a light aircraft, when there is a perfectly good airline service daily, from London into Zürich, which is much quicker?'

'It's because he's concerned that a terrorist attack may take place, either in the airport or on the aircraft.'

'Hmm...'

'... And, he has good reason to be alarmed after recent events!' I interrupted, and Boschert gave a nod. Then followed numerous questions, which I couldn't answer... and, it seemed the questioning was going around in circles, until I told him that I had been a squadron leader, flying missions in Afghanistan. Boschert's attitude changed, and he agreed to let us see Lu Ming.

After a phone call, the sergeant led us to an interview room, where Lu Ming was seated at a table. He looked composed and inscrutable, but managed a slight smile when we entered.

'... Ah, Cavendish... and mademoiselle.'

'How are you, sir?' I asked, as we sat opposite.

'As well as can be expected,' he replied, with a sigh.

'So, why are they holding you?'

'Because I've been doing business with a known arms dealer, who the Americans want deported, to face trial over there... and, the French also want him, on various charges connected with Algerian terrorists,' he replied, and my heart sank again.

'What sort of business, sir?'

'Mainly finance... and some other small interests,' he replied, and I couldn't help but wonder what these were.

'I see... and, is there any chance that you will be released soon, so we can return to England?' I asked forlornly.

'Possibly, but I must ask you stay here in Zürich until my release,' he replied, and I glanced at Hélène, who looked overjoyed at the prospect. I believe that when determined women decide to have their way, most men usually cave in... but, I was going to be resolute and steadfast... she would not succeed in tempting me to have sex with her!

After informing Captain Boschert that we would stay in Zürich until Lu Ming's release, we left the Gendarmerie to find a hotel. The Crown Plaza looked suitable so we booked in for two days, in single rooms. I made a call to Louise from my room, who was now quite angry at the further delay, while Hélène informed her father that we would be staying in Zürich.

We went down to the restaurant for a light lunch, and then decided to take a walk around the city. We talked about the possibility that as soon as Lu Ming was brought before a judge, that he would be free to leave the country, after posting bail. I was uncertain about this, and told Hélène that if he was held on remand, I would have to fly back to England, and await his release at home.

After dinner that evening, at the hotel, we returned to the Gendarmerie, to discover if there was any good news. Sergeant Amstutz politely informed us that Lu Ming would be in front of a judge tomorrow morning, and there was a strong possibility that he would be held on remand, due to the seriousness of the charges. I asked if we could attend the hearing; the sergeant informed us that we could, telling us when and where it would be held.

On our return to the hotel, we sat in the bar, and over several drinks of scotch, we made plans for the next day. I decided that I would only wait for one more day, before flying back home. Hélène agreed, and said she had to return her father's car, as she knew he was planning to go to Paris. We went up to our rooms, and I expected Hélène would make some amorous suggestion, but she didn't, which was a relief… so, we said 'bonne nuit' in the corridor, with a quick kiss on the cheek.

The next morning, after settling the hotel bill, we arrived at the court just before ten thirty, and sat waiting for the hearing to begin. The court filled up, and Lu Ming suddenly appeared in the dock, accompanied by a gendarme. Moments later the judge arrived, looking imperious in his sash, and gave a nod to the court, before taking his seat. The clerk read out the charges in German, which I didn't understand, but Hélène whispered her loose interpretation to me. It was alleged that Lu Ming had been financing terrorist activity in Algeria, through a Swiss bank, and was wanted in America for buying arms illegally. I knew that there was absolutely no chance of him being released, so made my plans to return home immediately. I whispered this to Hélène, who nodded, but looked disappointed. We waited until all the court formalities came to an end, to discover that Lu Ming would be held on remand. I made myself known to the notaire who represented Ming... I informed him who we were, and told him that I would now return to the UK and await developments. I gave him my card, and asked him to let his client know my intentions. The notaire thanked me, and we shook hands, before we left the courthouse.

Once outside I said, 'now, my lovely petite driver... take me straight to the airfield at Besancon please!'

'Oui, Pierre!'

We stopped at Luzern for coffee and fuel, before the final leg of the journey to the airfield, where Hélène gave me a passionate kiss, as we said 'au revoir'.

'I will see you again, won't I, Pierre?' she whispered.

'Of course, I'll be back to collect Lu Ming,' I replied, but thought that it might be some considerable time before that happened... and never, if he was extradited to America!

Hélène followed me to the tower, where I informed the air traffic controller that I was returning to the UK, and landing at Le Touquet, before crossing the Channel. He smiled and hoped that I had enjoyed flying in France... I just nodded.

Hélène kissed me once more, before I climbed into Papa Oscar and started up. She stood waving as I taxied out to the runway, and as departure clearance was given, I opened the throttle and quickly glanced back, to return the wave. Papa Oscar lifted effortlessly into the afternoon sky, and at a thousand feet, I set the reciprocal course for Reims. It was when I had adjusted the throttle to seventy five per cent engine speed for cruise, and watched the airspeed indicator slowly rise to one hundred knots, that I remembered that I was supposed to report to Chief Bosenquet, at the Gendarmerie! I thought, 'bugger the French!' and laughed.

I was flying home to Louise and the babes... and my peaceful, heavenly, safe farm!

CHAPTER 8

TROUBLE WITH LEISHA AND ROGER

It was dusk when I landed at my strip, and as I taxied up to the house, Louise appeared waving frantically. After shutting down, I climbed out and embraced my lovely wife.

'I'm so glad you're back, darling,' she said, as we made our way to the house, hand-in-hand.

'I know it's been a bit of an ordeal for you, when I kept phoning to say I'd been delayed, but when I tell you everything that's happened, I'm sure you'll understand.'

'I'm sure,' she smiled.

After the babes were put to bed, we had a late dinner, while I told her everything about my trip to France... including Hélène's involvement!

When I had finished, she asked, 'what do you think will happen now, to Lu Ming?'

'Well he could end up with a lengthy prison sentence, in Switzerland... or if he's deported to America, we'll never see him again.'

At that precise moment, my mobile rang... it was Roger!

'Hello, how are you, dear boy?'

'Fine thanks.'

'So, what have done with the Chinaman?' he asked, which took me back a little.

'How do you know?'

'Ah, Leisha said you'd flown off with him, to France... so, where is he now?'

'In prison, in Zürich,' I replied, and I heard Roger gasp.

'What the devil has he been up to?'

'Listen, I don't want to discuss this anymore, Roger.'

'Hmm... I suppose you don't really know who's listening...'

'...Precisely.'

'So, have you any idea how long he'll be in Zürich?'

'No, I haven't got a clue.'

'But it'll be awhile yet, don't you think?'

'…Possibly.'

'Good… I plan to spend some time with Leisha, getting to know her better.'

'I'm sure you know her quite well already!'

'Yes I do, but I want to refine certain things.'

'Like what? On second thoughts, don't tell me!'

'Yes, it's best you don't know, for the moment.'

'That's a relief!'

'Let's meet up for lunch soon… I've important things to discuss, and I need your sound advice.'

'…Alright… when and where?'

'…How about next Friday, at the Randolph in Oxford?'

'So, I guess you're staying with Leisha, at Witney?'

'I am indeed, and provided I'm not totally exhausted by her unbelievable tricks, if you know what I mean, I'll meet you next Friday.'

'I'll be there Roger.'

'Good, see you soon, dear boy,' he replied, before he rang off.

I glanced at Louise, gave a smile, and said, 'he's up to his neck in more women trouble.'

'…No change there then.'

'No… he can always be relied upon.'

'Well, don't you get yourself any more involved than you have to.'

'I promise.'

The next day I was with Bob, looking at the wheat in the top field, when my mobile rang.

'Hello.'

'Hi, Mr Cavendish, its Ralf Harwood here,' said the American, and my heart sank.

'…And, how can I help you today, Mr Harwood?'

'It's simple… by telling me why you flew Lu Ming to France?'

'Because he asked me to,' I replied, curtly.

'…And, why was that, Mr Cavendish?'

'Because he is afraid of flying by commercial airlines… as they, and the airports, are prone to terrorist attacks… as recent events prove.'

'Hmm... so you say, but we suspect that he was attempting to conceal his movements from the authorities.'

'Well, it's still a free country, so you can think what you like, Mr Harwood.'

'Mr Cavendish, you'd do well to co-operate with us, before things take a turn downwards for you...'

'Is that a threat, Mr Harwood?' I interrupted.

'...No, just friendly advice.'

'I'm glad to hear it... now, was there anything else?'

'...No, but we'll be in touch soon, Mr Cavendish... and, some more friendly advice would be *not to fly abroad*... especially to Switzerland... bye, Mr Cavendish!'

Bob looked at me, and asked, 'problems, boss?'

'Nothing I can't handle, Bob,' I replied... but, I was concerned.

The week passed by without anything happening, except a call from Hélène, saying that the gendarmes had questioned her about me and our trip into Switzerland. I told her not to worry, as she was completely innocent, and not involved in any way with Lu Ming. She sounded calm as we ended the call, but asked when I was next flying over to Besancon. I told her that I really didn't know, but I would come over as soon as I could, and she seemed happy with that. Then she sighed, and blew me a kiss before hanging up.

I flew up to Kidlington on the Friday morning, and after landing, I called Paula to see if she was free.

'Of course, Peter... I'll pop the kettle on, and we can have tea while you tell me all your news!'

'I'll call a taxi and be there soon, Paula.'

My lovely Aunt opened the door, and said, 'well this is a pleasant surprise, darling,' before she kissed me with a little too much passion. She led the way through to her kitchen, and as I sat at the table, she asked, 'so, what have you been up to?'

'You won't believe it, Paula,' I replied... she laughed, and said, 'try me!' So over tea and biscuits, I told her in detail about my flight to France with Lu Ming, and the adventures that followed in Switzerland. I also included Ralf Harwood in the story, and when I'd finished the tale, she looked dumbstruck, and whispered, 'dear God.'

'Quite... now, I think I'll need a good solicitor before much longer...'

'I'm certain of that, darling!' she interrupted.

'So, can you recommend one?'

'Of course... let me make a call to Martin James in London, he's utterly ruthless... and he hates all authority.'

'He sounds good to me.'

'Well, he is... but very expensive!'

'Don't worry about that.'

'I won't, because I'll settle his fee for you, darling.'

'Paula!'

'Not another word, I insist... now, I'm sure you didn't just fly up to see me, so what else have you planned?'

'I'm meeting Roger for lunch at the Randolph.'

'...And what does he want?'

'He says that he has things to discuss, and wants my advice.'

'That means he's up to his neck in woman trouble again!'

'I'm certain.'

'Well, let me know everything before you fly back today.'

'I will.'

'So, take my car, then you'll be sure to come back and tell me what he wants,' she said, with a smile. The curiousness of women passes every man's understanding!

I enjoyed driving Paula's sleek, black BMW to the Randolph in, where I parked in the customers' car park, and went in search of Roger. He was in the bar and looked haggard, but managed a smile, when he saw me. I guessed that Leisha had been giving him more sex than he could cope with, as he certainly looked completely knackered!

'Roger... how are you? But let me guess!'

'Do I look that bad?'

'Yes, you do... so, what's she done to you?'

'Oh dear God... she's divine, and I can't get enough of her!'

'Well, buy me a drink and tell all.'

He ordered an orange and tonic for me and a double scotch for himself, before we wandered over to a secluded table in the bar. As we sipped, he told me of the unbelievable and demanding sexual performance of Lu Ming's lovely wife. It appeared that she knew every possible trick to satisfy a man, time after time, until he was completely drained of everything... physically and mentally... and, Roger had almost lost the will to live, as he believed he was already in paradise!

'My God,' I whispered, as I knew this affair would only end in disaster!

'I love her, Peter... I really love her, and I can't live without her!' he said, and I feared for my friend's future.

'But, you're already married, Roger... so, what about Naomi and the baby?'

'I'm sorry, but can't do anything about them... I'll have to get divorced.'

'But, you must be sensible...'

'I can't!' he interrupted.

'Look Roger, if you carry on with this affair, you'll ruin your marriage, it'll finish your career and your life... because once Lu Ming finds out, and he will, you will be mincemeat!'

He shook his head, and replied, 'I know what you say is true, but I'll have to chance it.'

At that point I gave up, and said, 'well, if I can help you in any way, you only have to ask.'

'Thanks, Peter, you are a good pal.'

I sighed, and said, 'I know I am.' I knew that, somehow, he would embroil me in his disaster!

Over a delicious lunch of roast lamb, Roger took delight in telling me, in great detail, what sexy Leisha did to him, and herself, while he watched. I became quite hot under the collar at some of her unbelievable antics, and felt my loins stirring. Louise would certainly have a night to remember!

We said 'goodbye' outside the hotel, and promised to keep in touch, as things progressed. Roger returned to Leisha in Witney, while I drove back to Yarnton, to tell Paula the news.

After sitting in the lounge, I told her all about Roger's infatuation with the married beauty.

'He's a fool… and no mistake,' she said, emphatically.

'I know, and it'll end in disaster.'

'Can't he see that?'

'Obviously not… it seems she has some mystical power over him.'

'Well, he'll regret that… now, tell me what she does to him that is so compelling,' Paula said, with a smile.

I watched Paula getting more and more flushed as I continued to describe, in detail, Leisha's sexual antics with Roger, until she whispered, 'oh, Peter darling, please stop… I'm already very moist… and, now I need you to come upstairs and see to me.'

So, as Moll Flanders often asked, 'well… what would you do?'

The thought of having prolonged and wonderful sex with my voluptuous aunt was very appealing, but I knew I had to be true to my Louise; which made me whisper, 'I can't do it, Paula, I really can't.' She looked disappointed, shrugged her shoulders, and said, 'well, I had to ask.'

'Of course you did.'

'So, I think you'd better leave now, Peter.'

'I will,' I replied, and realised that she was now in a hurry to pleasure herself.

I took a taxi back to the airport, and flew back to the strip, knowing I had done the right thing, but wondered if I could resist Paula again, in different circumstances. After all, she was voluptuous and sexy… and, I guessed she knew tricks that could give immense pleasure… and, I think, describing Leisha's repertoire may have added to Paula's!

After a night of unbridled pleasure with Louise, which left her a little breathless at times, I felt that I was in a good place, and could cope with anything. In the morning, I strode out after breakfast and walked around the farm with Bob… and by the afternoon, it all changed!

First, Martin James, the solicitor, phoned and asked how he could assist me. After I told him I couldn't discuss the matter on the phone, he made an appointment for me to see him in two days, at his London office, in Chancery Lane. Within twenty minutes of that call, Paula phoned to ask if he'd been in contact, and after I said he had, she apologised for asking me to see to her intimate needs. I told her there was nothing to apologise for, but she said she was sorry… then, she added that I'm so sexy, and don't know it! I knew that, in the future, it might be very difficult for me to keep my hands off this lovely woman!

It was an hour later that Leisha phoned.
'Peter, help me… they've taken him away!' she sobbed.
'…Who?'
'Roger…. two Americans came to the house just now, and took him away…'
'…Where to, Leisha?' I interrupted, with concern.
'I don't know, but I think they've taken him to London,' she replied.
'Did they give their names?'
'I think I heard one say he was Ralf something-or-other.'
'Ralf Harwood?'
'Yes… I think so… but, I'm confused… why do they want him?'
'Perhaps to discover if Roger is involved with your husband.'
'Well, he's not.'
'I know that…'
'Please help him, Peter.'
'I'll try and find out where they've taken him.'
'… And, let me know as soon as you can.'
'I promise I will,' I said, with a heavy heart, as I knew this might prove difficult.
'Thank you, Peter, you're a good friend,' she said, before she ended the call. Everyone tells me 'I'm a good friend… and sexy with it', but it certainly wasn't allowing me to lead a quiet life!

I went back into the house to talk to Louise, and try to formulate some sort of plan, to help Roger. I was in the middle of telling Louise the news, when Naomi phoned to ask if Roger was with me… she hadn't seen him for days! Dear God, this was all getting very tricky! I tried to placate Naomi, but without much success… she blazed away about him, before she ended the call with threats to cut his bollocks off, when he eventually arrived home! Which was a worry, but my friend was the architect of his own disaster, and I was determined to try and help him… if I could. After I finished telling Louise the complete story, she suggested that she called her old boss, Inspector Halliday, at Weymouth Police Station. She would ask if he could help, by contacting the Thames Valley Police at Oxford, in the hope that they would share their information. It was a long shot, but worth a try, so Louise phoned the Inspector. After pleasantries, Louise told him the story, and he promised to make inquiries and get back to her.

We didn't hear anything from him until the next morning. He told Louise that he was unable to shed any light on the arrest, and presumed it was an operation carried out by American security. Louise thanked him, and we were now at a loss to know what to do… so, I decided to call Ralf Harwood. I found his business card and phoned.
'Mr Harwood… it's Peter Cavendish…'
'Hi, Mr Cavendish… how are you doing today?'
'Fine thanks… now, I'm making enquiries about my friend Roger Burton, and I think you might know where he is.'
'I certainly do, Mr Cavendish.'
'So, where is he?'
'He's safe.'
'…But where?'
'I just told you… he's with us and he's okay.'
'His wife is concerned…'
'I bet she is!' he interrupted.
'Well, can she see him?'
'Not at the moment, but all in good time, Mr Cavendish… thanks for the call,' he said abruptly, before hanging up.
I told Louise then called Naomi, who was not impressed, and said, 'God only knows what he's been up to now, and when I find out… he's toast!'
I said 'goodbye' as empathically as I could, and she snapped

back, 'bye!'

I was unsure how I could help Roger, and decided to think about the situation overnight... but in the meantime, I called Leisha and told her that Roger was safe and with the Americans. She asked so many questions that I had no answer for, but promised that as soon as I knew more, I'd contact her.

The next afternoon, I was due to meet Martin James, but just before I set off on my journey to London, my mobile rang persistently.

'Hello... Cavendish here.'

'Ah, Monsieur Cavendish... this is Pascal Gerrard, Monsieur Lu Ming's notaire speaking.'

'Bonjour Monsieur... do you have some good news?' I asked, anxiously.

'Monsieur Lu Ming has been subjected to an International arrest warrant. He will soon be extradited to Britain, and he has asked me to inform you,' he replied.

'Well thank you... do you know when he will arrive back?'

'No, Monsieur, but I will call you again when he is due to leave Zürich.'

'Thank you... do you know if any further charges have been made?'

'No, Monsieur, there are no further allegations against him.'

'Well, that's a relief!'

'I will be in touch, Monsieur.'

'Thank you... goodbye.'

I drove to London with my mind full of questions and feared that I would need Martin James' help, if I was to survive the strong possibility of being caught up in Lu Ming's illegal activities. I parked the Bentley in the underground car park at Marble Arch, and took the Underground to Chancery Lane. On arrival, I was shown into Martin James' office and announced by an attractive receptionist, as he stood to greet me from behind a paper-strewn desk. James was about my age, smartly dressed and had the look of a strong and talented man, behind his piercing blue eyes. No wonder that Paula thought he was the cat's pyjamas!

'Mr Cavendish… I'm pleased to meet you,' he said with a smile, as he waved me to sit.

'Thanks.'

'Now, your aunt has told me a little of your problems, so would you like to elaborate?'

'Indeed I would,' I replied, and proceeded to tell him everything. After I'd regaled him with my saga, he discussed various means by which I could untangle myself. He also advised that he would engage a leading barrister, to defend me in court… should that be necessary… and, I thought that was very probable!

I left his office just as the rush hour began, and had to fight my way onto the Underground, amongst all the tired office workers, and thought how lucky I was to live on my lovely farm. The traffic out of London was slow and it took me some time to reach the motorway, where I could allow the Bentley to cruise, at speed, towards Devon.

Arriving home, Louise was full of questions, which I tried my best to answer, but I could see that she was very worried… as was I. We spent a restless night, and I wondered what the hell was going to happen next… and, I didn't have to wait long!

CHAPTER 9

WHAT NEXT, I WONDER?

Two days later, Roger arrived at the farm. I was making my way down to Papa Oscar, when I heard a car roar into the yard. I turned around to see him at the wheel of his sleek BMW, and thought, 'oh dear God, he's now free from the Yanks, so whatever next?'
I strode up to greet him as he left the car, looking pale, and he gave me a half-hearted smile.

'Roger... what a surprise.'

'Hello Peter... I'm in a hell of a mess... and, you're the only one who can help me now.'

I sighed, and replied, 'then come into the house and tell all...'

'I'd prefer to take a walk outside,' he interrupted.

'Okay... let's have a gentle stroll up to the top meadow,' I replied, wondering what my friend was about to tell me, that I didn't know already.

He took a deep breath, and said, 'I've just come from seeing Leisha...she's had a phone call from her husband's notaire in Zürich, telling her that Lu Ming will be extradited soon to Britain... and, I'm terrified!'

'... And, so you should be... I bloody told you!'

'I know, I know... but, I can't resist this woman.'

'So, what are you going to do?'

'Ask your advice... and, while I make plans, stay here with you and Louise,' he replied.

'...Oh really?'

'Yes... and, when you hear what's happened to me, you'll realise why.'

'Well, I'm all ears, Roger.'

'When I was staying with Leisha, some American agents came to the house and arrested me...'

'I know, Leisha called and told me...'

'... And, did you do anything?' he interrupted.

'Yes, Louise phoned her old boss and he made inquiries with Thames Valley Police, but he said he could find nothing about your arrest… so, I visited the embassy, and was told they had you in custody and you were safe, but they wouldn't let me see you.'

'Well, thanks for that…these bloody Americans are ruthless…'

'I can believe that!'

'They said if I didn't co-operate I would face rendition back to the States!'

'Thank God that you obviously did the right thing then, otherwise we would have never seen you again.'

'I know.'

'…So, what now?'

'I need to stay here and think for a while.'

'Does Naomi know where you are?'

'No…'

'Don't you think you should tell her?'

'Not at the moment…'

'Roger, you have a worried wife, who is pregnant, so surely you need to put her mind at rest?'

'I'll have to think about that.'

'Well, if you don't tell her, I will.'

He glared at me, and said, 'I thought you were my friend!'

'I am, but it's only fair that you tell her where you are.'

'Hmm… I suppose so…. But, I need to hide, Peter.'

'Well you can't hide here…'

'…Why not?' he interrupted.

'Because the Americans have been here already, and after I called them to find out where you were, Harwood left me in no doubt he'd be in touch again!'

'…Oh my God!'

'Quite… now, I think I know somewhere you could hide for the present.'

'…Where?'

'Well, provided you let Naomi know, I'll ask Paula if you can stay with her,' I replied, and he looked relieved.

'Thanks Peter.'

'…And, make sure you tell no one, except Naomi.'

'Okay.'

'…And Leisha!'

'Alright, alright,' he said, testily.

'Give me a moment to call Paula, and if she agrees, I'll fly you up to Kidlington.'
'What about my car?'
'I'll hide it…'
'…Where?'
'Don't you worry, it'll be safe,' I assured him.

Paula agreed without any hesitation, and after some tea and sympathy from Louise, Roger called Naomi and tried to placate her… but he wasn't successful. An hour later we took off in Papa Oscar for Kidlington, before taking a taxi out to Yarnton. Paula greeted us like long lost lovers and kissed with gusto, before leading us into the lounge.

'So, tell me everything,' she said with a smile, as she slumped down on the settee. Roger told her his tale of woe, with me adding little snippets of information, while Paula looked sympathetic, until he had finished.

'Well, Roger dear, you can stay with me as long as you like,' she said with a smile, while I hoped that she would not entice him into sexual adventures! I thought that he'd had enough of those already, but Paula might want to try some of her tricks on him!

After promising to stay in touch with any developing news, and kissing Paula 'goodbye,' I flew back to the strip feeling uneasy. As the green countryside drifted slowly beneath my wings, I wondered if I had endangered my aunt by involving her with Roger. The American agents or Lu Ming's thugs could find her if they really tried, and heaven only knows what would be the result. After landing, I went into the house and told Louise everything that had been worrying me. We sat and talked for some time, before Louise said that we would just have to wait and see what happened next; then take the appropriate action. My clever wife suggested we should park Roger's BMW in her parents' garage, as they were away in Spain, for two weeks holiday… and, by the time they arrived home, Roger would have hopefully collected the car. This was done before dinner that evening.

The next morning a letter arrived from Martin James, setting out my legal position, and it concluded by telling me that he had engaged a formidable barrister, by the name of Rupert Brackenbury. I only felt vaguely comfortable with this, as I realised that things could get very tricky from now on… and, they did!

I wondered what was going to happen next, and I didn't have to wait long. A day later, a black Jaguar swept into the yard, almost knocking me over, and two men climbed out.

'Mr Peter Cavendish?' asked the older one.

'Yes.'

'I'm Superintendent Morton and this is Inspector Freeman, we're from the Serious Crime Unit at New Scotland Yard,' he said firmly, and my mind went into free-fall.

'So, how can I help you gentlemen?' I managed to ask, knowing full well what it was all about.

'May we go somewhere private, sir?' asked Morton.

'Yes, please come into the house,' I replied, and led them through the kitchen, where I whispered to Louise, 'police,' then to my study, and waved them to sit.

'So, what's this all about, gentlemen?'

'We know that you've had dealings with a Chinese businessman, named Lu Ming.'

'Yes, that is so, Superintendent.'

'Would you mind telling us exactly what those dealings were, sir?' he asked, as Freeman took out his notebook. Have you noticed that the police are so achingly polite, when they are just about to accuse you of some dreadful crime?

'He asked me to fly him to France.'

'…And why was that, sir?'

'…Because he doesn't like flying with any of the airlines.'

'Why is that, sir?'

'Because Mr Ming believes that the planes, and the airports, are vulnerable to terrorist attack,' I replied, and I could see that they didn't believe a word of it.

'…And did Mr Ming know of any planned terrorist attack?' he asked, and I knew that we were now on dangerous ground.

'No, no, he didn't… it was just the fear of it.'

'Hmm... I see.'

'Well, I wonder if you do, Superintendent,' I said, but before he could answer, I continued... 'some people are very scared of flying, and added to that there is the fear of a terrorist outrage, which your commissioner of The Met has repeatedly said on television, 'it's not if... it's when.' This took them back for a moment, and I was pleased that my outburst had struck home.

'Well, sir...' began Morton, but I interrupted him,

'...Let me be clear, Superintendent, my business with Mr Lu Ming has been entirely legal, so there is nothing to answer... and, I fear you've had a wasted journey!'

'Mr Cavendish, let me also be clear... Mr Ming has been arrested in Zürich, and I think you know why, and that makes you a person of interest to us and the Swiss authorities,' he said firmly.

'...Oh really?'

'Yes, sir... now, please tell us what you know about Mr Lu Ming's activities... and, leave nothing out.'

I remained silent for a few moments, while gathering my thoughts, before replying, 'I was contacted by Mr Ming, after a friend had advised him that I was an experienced pilot, who owned a light aircraft. He invited me to his home in Grosvenor Square, to discuss the possibility of flying him over to France.'

'... And, you knew that he'd crossed the border into Switzerland?'

'I did, but only after he had done so... and, he'd had the accident on his way back to Besancon.'

'... And, what did you do then?'

'After being advised by the local gendarmerie of the crash, I, along with a helpful lady, drove to the hospital in Berne, to discover his condition, as any reasonable person would do.'

'Quite so, sir... and, we know that you are aware that Mr Ming has been accused of criminal activity, regarding the financing of arms dealing...'

'Yes, I do, after his notaire phoned me from Zürich,' I interrupted.

'Do you know anything about this, sir?'

'No, Superintendent, I don't,' I replied... and, he glanced at Freeman, who gave a slight nod.

Morton looked serious, as he said, 'Mr Cavendish, I'd like you to come back to London for further questioning.'

'Why should I? I've done nothing wrong!'

'Sir, if you don't agree to come voluntarily, then I will arrest you,' he said calmly. At that moment Louise walked in, and asked, 'would you gentlemen like some coffee?'

Morton was taken aback by the interruption, and replied, 'no thank you, madam.'

'Are you sure?' she persisted.

'...Quite sure.'

'...And what about you?' she asked Freeman, with a smile.

'No thanks.'

'... And you, Peter?'

'Yes please, darling... I'll need something before I go up to London, with these officers,' I said, and Morton looked relieved.

'London?'

'Yes.'

'Will you be long?' Louise asked, with concern.

'I don't think so, darling.'

'Well, thank heavens for that... you're not a criminal!'

'I know, but these chaps don't know that!' I replied with a smile... but, I was still concerned.

Half an hour later, we left in the Jaguar; with me sitting in the back with Morton, while Freeman drove at speed. I estimated that he was driving at well over eighty miles an hour on some stretches of open road. It was as we were approaching Weymouth, that I suddenly noticed blue flashing lights, reflected in the rear view mirror.

'Oh Christ!' said Freeman.

'What's the matter?' asked Morton.

'I've picked up a traffic car,' he replied, as the Jaguar slowed and eventually stopped.

'Dear God,' whispered Morton, as a uniformed officer arrived at the driver's door. Freeman touched the window remote, and I chuckled, as I knew this was going to be tricky for the detectives... the biter bit!

'Hello, sir,' said the policeman.

'Hello, officer.'

'Do you know why I've stopped you, sir?'

'Why don't you tell me?' said Freeman sarcastically, as he produced his warrant card and showed it to the policeman, who took out of his hand.

'Hey!'

'Inspector James Freeman, Metropolitan Police... so, that's you, is it, sir?'

'It certainly is!'

'Then you should know better...'

'We're on official police business officer,' interrupted Freeman, as my passenger door opened and another office appeared, and asked, 'would you please identify yourselves?'

'Certainly,' I replied with a smile, 'I'm Peter Cavendish of Long Meadow Farm,' I said, as I produced my driving licence. The officer glanced at it and gave it back.

'... And you, sir?'

'I'm Superintendent Morton, of the Serious Crime Unit, New Scotland Yard,' replied Morton, as he produced his warrant card.

'Thank you, sir.'

'Why have you stopped us officer?' asked Morton.

'Because you were driving at excessive speed, and endangering other road users, by overtaking while being head on to oncoming traffic, sir.'

'That's ridiculous!'

'This unmarked vehicle was travelling between ninety-two and ninety-five miles an hour, while head on to other traffic... we have it all on camera, sir,' replied the officer, and Morton didn't know what to say.

I thought, 'this is good! So what happens next? Will Freeman be arrested?'

The officer at Freeman's window asked for his driving licence, and then said, 'have you any points, sir?'

'Yes, six, if you must know!' replied Freeman, and the officer raised his eyebrows.

'I will have to report you for excessive speeding and reckless driving, sir.'

'Is that really necessary, officer?' asked Morton.

'Oh, yes indeed, sir... we have a duty to keep the roads safe for all users...'

'But dammit, man, we're on official police business!' interrupted Morton, angrily.

'So, are you now telling me that you are on an emergency call, sir?'

'...No, of course not!'

'Then you should know that the speed limit is sixty miles an hour... and, your driver was well in excess of ninety!'

'But officer...'

'They are no 'buts' sir... it will be for senior officers to decide what action to take about these offences.'

'Oh God,' whispered Morton.

I wanted to say that, 'no one is above the law,' but thought better of it, so just smiled.

Within moments it was all over, and the policemen disappeared from view. As we resumed our journey, I noticed Freeman glancing in the rear view mirror, saying with malice, 'bloody country bumpkins!'

'Now, Inspector, they're only doing their job,' said Morton... Freeman sighed, and gave a nod. There was only a little conversation between them throughout the journey to New Scotland Yard, and I guessed that Freeman would be charged with driving offences, and his chief could do little to protect him... after all, it was all on camera!

After arriving at the Met's headquarters, I was taken to an interview room and left alone. I presumed Morton and Freeman were getting their notes together, and I decided to go on the attack. As soon as they entered the room and switched on the tape, I waited until Morton asked, 'are you Peter Cavendish of Long Meadow Farm, Dorset?'

'I am... and, I have come here voluntarily to help you with your inquiries, concerning the activities of a Chinese businessman, Mr Lu Ming; who I flew to France recently, as he is very concerned about flying with all the airlines, because of the threat of terrorist attacks...'

'So you said, sir,' interrupted Morton, but before he could say anything else, I continued...

'...And furthermore, as a retired Royal Air Force squadron leader, I believe that my loyalty to Queen and country is clear... and my wife, who was a police officer, proves that we are law abiding citizens!'

'Mr Cavendish...' began Morton.

'... And, before I answer any more of your questions, I tell you now that I am completely innocent of any wrong doing, and wish to contact my solicitor!' I interrupted, and they both looked deflated.

'Of course, Mr Cavendish... you can make the call from Inspector Freeman's office,' replied Morton.

I made the call, and Martin James was with me half an hour later. Morton questioned me relentlessly, but I had a believable answer every time, and when there was any doubt, James interrupted forcefully with, 'you don't have to answer that.' At last the interrogation ended and I was free to go, but I made the point to Morton that I had come voluntarily to London, and I would not return... unless I was under arrest.

Outside New Scotland Yard, I thanked Martin for all his assistance, and caught a cab to Paddington. On the train back to Weymouth, the slow journey gave me a chance to consider the events of the day, and make some plans for future dramas... which I was sure would follow!

Arriving home by taxi, I wandered into the house and kissed Louise. Over dinner, I told her everything, and when I had finished, she just said, 'well, that was all a waste of time!'

That night I slept very little, worrying about my involvement with Lu Ming... but, had I known what was to follow, I wouldn't have slept at all!

CHAPTER 10

SURPRISING EVENTS

The next two days passed quickly, without any interruptions to my farm activities, and then on day three, Roger called.

'Hello old chap... how are you?'

'Okay I think, Roger... you alright?'

'Yes thanks.'

'... And, how's Paula?'

'Oh she's as lovely as ever.'

'I hope you're behaving yourself!'

'Of course, I am... now, I need my car because I've decided to go home and face the music... so, would you come and collect me as soon as possible?'

His request took me back a little, but I replied, 'yes of course... I'll fly up to Kidlington after lunch.'

'Thanks Peter.'

'I'll call you as I leave... and, perhaps Paula will drive you to the airport to meet me.'

'I'll ask her, but I'm sure it will be okay... she is always so obliging,' he said, which made me wonder if he had behaved himself at all with my lovely aunt... and, I would ask him.

I landed at Kidlington just before three, and as I taxied Papa Oscar from the runway, I noticed Paula's BMW parked near the control tower. Roger stepped from the car, as I shut down the aircraft, then he strolled over to meet me.

'I'm glad you're here, Peter.'

'You sound concerned,' I replied, climbing down from the cockpit.

'Yes, I am... I must get home to Naomi as soon as I can...'

'Has something happened?' I interrupted.

'Yes, I called her, and she's had a visit from the bloody Yanks...'

'... And, what did they want?' I asked, but guessed.

'To know where I was, but she told them she didn't know... or care!' he replied.

'Hmm, so what will you tell her when you get home?' I asked.

'That I was with you,' he replied, and at that moment Paula joined us.

'Take him home, darling… he needs some TLC,' she said with a smile, but I knew that Naomi was unlikely to give him any tender loving care.

'Of course… I'll just pay the landing fee, and then we'll be off,' I said, with a nod.

'Good… and, call me when you get back to the farm… I want to know you're both okay,' Paula said, and I guessed she wanted to talk to me about Roger.

During the flight back, Roger only commented on the green, rolling countryside beneath our wings, and said nothing about his stay with Paula… but, I was anxious to know everything, and would question him on landing. After a smooth flight, I landed and taxied to a halt at the end of the strip, shut down, and we both climbed out from the cockpit.

'So, tell me Roger, how did you get on with Paula?'

'Oh, very well… she's such a good listener.'

'… So, what did you tell her?'

He sighed, and replied, 'I told her that I'm leaving Naomi.'

'… And, what did she say?'

'She said I was a fool, and should think carefully before I did anything rash.'

'So, have you?'

'Yes, I've made up my mind to divorce Naomi… so I'll be free to be with Leisha.'

I shook my head, and said, 'dear God, Roger, I think you're mad!'

'Possibly, but that's the way it is… shall we go in?'

'Yes, okay,' I replied, with a sigh.

'I'm dying for a cup of tea,' he said, before striding off towards the house, which left any questioning about his conduct with Paula hanging in the air.

After tea and some more sympathy from Louise, I drove Roger to

Louise's parents' house, to collect his BMW. We said 'goodbye,' and promised to keep in touch, before he accelerated away; back to London to tell his wife their marriage was over... and, I despaired. I could see that Roger's involvement with Leisha would inevitably end in tragedy... and, I was not wrong!

I called Paula later, and we had a long chat about Roger... she had given up, just as I had!

Later that evening, Leisha phoned me to ask if I knew where Roger was, and I told her that he had gone home to see his wife. She seemed relieved, which was surprising; then told me that her husband was now back in London, as he had been released on bail.

'I'm going to our house in Grosvenor Square, to see him tonight, and find out what's been going on,' she said, firmly.

'Please give your husband my regards, and tell him that the police have interviewed me about his business activities in Zürich... but, I told them that I knew nothing, and only flew him to France, at his request.'

'Thank you, Mr Cavendish... I'll tell him, and I'm sure he will be grateful.'

'I'm sure... and, please remind him he still owes me for the flight.'

'No doubt he will be in touch with you soon,' she replied, before we said 'goodbye.'

The next morning I was in my study, when Natasha called.

'Peter darling, how are you?' on hearing her voice, my spine shivered.

'Fine thanks... and, how are you?'

'I'm okay, but I need to see you again...'

'I don't think that's a good idea, Natasha,' I interrupted.

'But, you don't know why I need to see you, darling.'

'I can guess!'

'Well, you're bloody wrong!'

'...Oh really?'

'Yes!'

'So, what's this all about?'

'I know that you flew Lu Ming to France...'

'How do you know that?' I interrupted.

'…Because he told me!'

'He told you?'

'Yes, he phoned me last night, and told me the whole story, darling.'

'Did he now?'

'Yes… and, you're in big trouble!'

'Tell me something I don't know!'

'Listen… meet me as soon as you can…'

'Not until I know what it's about!'

'I'll tell you when I see you, darling… so, do be quick.'

I sighed, as I knew any resistance was futile, and asked, 'so where and when this time, Natasha?'

'Let's meet tomorrow morning at the Crown Hotel, in Abingdon, as usual,' she replied.

'Okay, I'll be there about eleven.'

'Good… and, don't tell anyone!' she said before hanging up, which left me wondering what was going on now.

That evening, I told Louise that I was going to meet Natasha, in Abingdon… she was not best pleased, but understood and shared my fears.

'The sooner you get everything sorted out, and finish with this bloody Lu Ming, the better!'

'…Of course.'

'…And, I blame Roger for involving you in his craziness, which will all end in disaster… just you wait and see!'

'I'm sure you're right.'

On the journey up to Abingdon, all manner of questions cascaded through my mind, and this time I was determined to get the truth, from Natasha. I arrived just before eleven, parked the Bentley nearby, and made my way into the hotel. I spotted Natasha waiting in reception…. she looked lovely.

'Hello, darling,' she purred, as she stood to kiss me.

'Natasha, it's good to see you again,' I said, and curiously meant it.

'… And you, darling… will you order some coffee?'

'Of course,' I replied, and signalled to a passing waiter.

While we waited to be served, I asked, 'so what's this all about, Natasha?'

'It's a long story, and I haven't been entirely truthful with you, Peter.'

'Now, there's a surprise!'

'... And, I'm very sorry about that...' she hesitated for a moment.

'Well, go on then.'

'I told you that Lu Ming occasionally came to my house at Wallingford, to watch me with Igor.'

'Yes, you did.'

'In fact, we became close and he invited me up to London... and, we stayed at the Savoy for a few days.'

'Hmm... I'm not surprised.'

'... And, it's so wonderful having sex with a man who has imagination, and takes his time.'

'Well, I wouldn't know,' I said with a grin, and she laughed.

'Of course not, darling... and, after our little stay at the Savoy, he asked me to move in to one of his luxury flats... he owns a block of them, you know?'

'I didn't know, but do go on.'

'Well, I'm very reluctant to leave my house here and move to London, because of Tim and Chris... I would miss them so much... it's their sheer physical vitality that's so rewarding.'

'Of course, you would miss them,' I said, as the sight of Natasha being pounded into sublime ecstasy by these two very fit, sex gluttons, flashed into my mind once more.

'... And, now comes the tricky part... his wife has found out about me,' she said, angrily.

'...Oh, dear.'

'You could say that, darling, but it gets even more complicated,' she said, as the waiter arrived with the coffee.

After he had left us, I said, 'well carry on, Natasha... I'm all ears.'

'Not here, darling, because we might be overheard, I'd rather tell you all about it in your car... is it nearby?'

I smelled a rat, but agreed to listen to her sordid tale of sex with

the Chinaman, and replied, 'yes, it's parked quite close.'
'Good, we'll finish our coffee first.'

Ten minutes later, we left the hotel, walked to the Bentley, and as I opened the passenger door for her, she said, 'this is a lovely car darling.'

'Yes... isn't it just?'

'You can take me for a long ride anytime you like!'

'Not now, Natasha,' I replied abruptly, as she slipped onto the front seat and I closed the door. As I sat in the driver's seat beside her, she sighed, and said, 'darling, I'm now very frightened...'

'...What about?' I interrupted.

'Just about everything at the moment, and what's going to happen next,' she replied.

'Well, tell me then.'

'I think Lu is going to murder his wife, and then get you to dispose of her,' she said, anxiously.

'Dear God,' I whispered.

'... And, then he'll kill you!'

'Why ever would he want to do that?' I asked... now feeling very frightened, as I knew his thugs could easily murder me.

'Because only you know where you'll bury her on your farm, and if the police ever found her body, they will trace it all back to him,' she replied.

'So, how will the police know?'

'After Lu has murdered you, he will tell them that you were having an affair with his wife, and she's now disappeared somewhere abroad, with you.'

'My God,' I whispered.

'He's very clever at arranging such things, darling.'

'I'm sure he is.'

'...And, they will never find your body.'

'How do you know all this, Natasha?'

'Because he hints that it would be convenient if his wife wasn't here anymore... and, he told me that she has taken millions from his Hong Kong bank, and he is determined to get the money back,' she replied.

'So, revenge would be his motive for killing her?'

'Yes, of course… and, with her out of the way, he could recover his money.'

'Would it be that easy?'

'Listen, darling, he knows powerful men in finance, who would help him.'

I sighed, and said, 'yes I'm sure he does.'

'So, I've joined up all the dots and figured out what might happen.'

'But, you don't know for sure, do you?'

'No, but I've got a pretty good idea that is what he intends,' she replied.

'Well, judging by recent events, he's likely to be sent to prison for a long time, so he can't do much from there.'

'Possibly, but I think he'll murder her and then you, before he faces a trial… and, he's got plenty of money to hire the best barristers, so he may get off… think about that!'

My heart sank, and I began to sweat, as I realised what a dreadful spider's web I was now trapped in! Bugger Roger… he started all this!

'Does he know about my friend, Roger?' I asked.

'I don't think so, darling… why do you ask?'

'Because he's busy screwing Leisha at the moment,' I replied.

'Is that really true?'

'It is.'

'Well, when Lu finds out, your friend Roger will be on his little list, for your disposal… make no mistake!'

'Dear God Almighty… is there no end to this?' I whispered.

'It seems not, darling.'

I tried to think of a plan of escape, and asked, 'so, when do you think he'll murder his wife and Roger, and then come after me?'

'I don't know, but soon after I've told him about not moving into his flat, darling.'

'How long can you keep him waiting?'

She shrugged her shoulders, and replied, 'probably a couple of weeks, before I say 'no' to him.'

'So, I've got just two weeks to plan something.'

'Yes, but he will have to dispose of Leisha first, and then Roger before he does anything to you.'

'Well, I suppose that's a small comfort,' I said, and she nodded.

I gave a sigh, and asked, 'so, is there anything else you can tell me, Natasha?'

'No, darling… not at the moment… but, I'll let you know if I find out anything else.'

'Thanks… so, I think I'll go home, and try to plan what I'll do next.'

'That's a good idea, darling… but, let me know your plans, and perhaps I can help you.'

I nodded, gave her a quick kiss on the cheek, and opened the door to get out, but she pulled me back and gave me a long, lingering kiss on the lips… which I did enjoy!

I drove home in a quiet and sombre mood, with my mind full of unanswered questions. *Was Natasha really telling me the truth, or was it all made up? Should I tell Roger, and ask for police protection for us both… and, what about the American Agents?* I would find out in time… heaven help me!

After arriving home, I told Louise everything… but, left out the more sordid details.

'If what this woman says is true, then you'll need help, darling… this man is a monster!' she said, emphatically.

'…So, what do you suggest?'

'Go to the police, and tell them everything… but, say that this deranged woman may be making it all up.'

'Hmm… I don't want to do or say anything that causes more problems than it solves.'

'Don't be silly… do as I say, and go to the police!'

'Right… so, should I tell Roger?'

'Of course… he must be warned.'

I went to my study and phoned Superintendent Morton's direct line, at New Scotland Yard.

'It's Peter Cavendish here, Superintendent.'

'Hello, Mr Cavendish… how can I help you today?'

'I have some important information, and I'd like to come and talk to you.'

'Is it concerning Lu Ming?'

'…Yes, Superintendent.'

'How soon can you be here, sir?'

I glanced at my watch, and replied, 'if I leave home now, then I can be with you at about five o'clock.'

'I look forward to seeing you then, sir… goodbye.'

'Goodbye, Superintendent.'

I next called Roger, and he sounded quite well, greeting me with a cheery, 'hello.'

'Hello Roger… its Peter.'

'So, how are you dear boy?'

'Okay… and you?'

'…On top of the world!'

'That's good to hear… now, I need to talk to you…'

'… And, I want to talk to you too!' he interrupted.

'Where are you now?'

'At home, packing,' he replied.

'…Packing?'

'Yes… and, I'll tell you everything when we meet.'

'Well, I'll be in London this evening, so shall we meet up?'

'Oh, yes… how about dinner at eight, at 'El Roma' in Harrow?'

'That will be great… see you then, Roger… bye.'

'Bye, dear boy.'

My friend sounded in high spirits, so obviously something good had happened… and, I couldn't help but wonder what it was. Hopefully, my bad news over dinner at 'El Roma', his favourite Italian restaurant, wouldn't dampen his outlook too much!

After telling Louise my arrangements for the rest of the day, we kissed, and she wished me, 'good luck, darling.'

The Bentley propelled me up to London with consummate ease, and the journey allowed me to mentally prepare myself. I parked in the underground car park at Marble Arch, and then took the Underground, arriving at New Scotland Yard just before five. After telling the officer at reception the purpose of my visit, I was quickly shown up to an interview room, and asked to wait. It wasn't long before Superintendent Morton arrived, with Inspector Freeman.

'Good afternoon, Mr Cavendish,' said Morton, as he sat opposite me. Freeman gave a nod in my direction, before he sat next to Morton, and he switched on the tape. Freeman gave the time and interview details, before I said, 'good afternoon, gentlemen.'

'So, what brings you to Scotland Yard, sir?' asked Morton.

I took a deep breath, and replied, 'I want to inform you that it is probable that Lu Ming may murder his wife… and then me!'

They looked suitably shocked, and Morton asked, 'how do you know this, sir?'

'Because this morning I met Mrs Natasha Templeton at a hotel in Abingdon, she is a well- connected lady and was a close friend of Charles Macmillan, the Government Minister who was murdered in London last year… and, she is now is a friend of Lu Ming, Superintendent.'

Morton raised his eyebrows and glanced at Freeman, who looked surprised.

'Go on, if you please, sir,' said Morton, and I then told them everything that Natasha had said, but left out my disposal of Leisha's body!

After I'd finished my tale of impending murders, Morton asked if I wanted police protection, but I said 'no,' for the present. He said that they would make further discreet inquiries about Mrs Templeton, without alerting her, and keep in close contact with me. I was grateful and left the detectives to make their plans. As I stepped out from New Scotland Yard, I felt relieved, and looked forward to seeing Roger at eight, for dinner.

I stopped at Starbucks for a leisurely coffee, before taking the Underground back to Marble Arch. I then drove the Bentley into Hyde Park, where I stopped, to call Louise. She was pleased to hear that my interview went well, and that we could count on the help of the police, if needed.

'…So, I wonder what dear Roger will have to tell you over dinner tonight,' said Louise, in a curious tone.

'Probably that he's about to run away with Leisha!'

'Well nothing that silly fool does, would surprise me!'

'No… me neither… I'll see you later, darling.'

'Okay… and, please don't be too late, will you?'

'No… I promise.'

I arrived at 'El Roma' at eight, and found Roger at the bar with a large scotch. He positively beamed when he saw me, and said, 'hello dear boy… what'll you have?'

'Hello Roger… an orange and tonic, please.'

'Ah, yes, you're driving the big beast!'

'I am… and, I'm going straight home after dinner.'

'Good man… now, shall I tell you my wonderful news first?' he asked.

'…Why not?' I replied, before he ordered my drink.

We said, 'cheers' and clinked glasses, as he took a deep breath, and said, 'I've left Naomi… she's gone to her parents, God help them… and, I'm going away with Leisha tomorrow.'

'Roger, have you really thought this through?'

'I have… and, it's for the best…'

'…*Whose best,* Roger?' I interrupted.

'Mine and Leisha's, dear boy… you don't know what's happened…'

'I think I do!'

'Lu Ming wants to divorce Leisha, because he's now involved with that Templeton woman… he wants her to move into one of his flats.'

'So I believe… but, according to Natasha Templeton, Lu Ming intends to murder his wife… then you… and, after I've disposed of your bodies… me too!'

'Good God Almighty!' he exclaimed, in total shock.

'…Precisely.'

'I don't believe it!'

'Oh Roger… please.'

'When did she tell you this?'

'This morning… and, then I came up to Scotland Yard, and

told the police.'

'So, what did they say?'

'They'll make discreet inquiries…'

'Which means they'll do nothing!' he interrupted, as a waiter approached and said, 'your table is ready, sir.'

We went through into the busy restaurant, and sat at a table for two in a corner, which was best for discreet conversation. After glancing through the menu, I chose fillet steak and Roger chose Coq au vin. He gave the order to the waiter, and after he left us, asked, 'so when does this wretched Chinaman intend to kill us?'

'Natasha says that it'll happen after she tells him that she won't be moving into his flat… she says she can keep him guessing for about two weeks,' I replied.

'Two weeks?'

'Yes.'

'Well, Leisha and I are going off tomorrow… and, he'll never find us,' said Roger, triumphantly.

'Where are you going?'

'I think it's best I don't tell you, dear boy… just phone me if you want to talk,' he replied.

I raised my eyebrows, and said, 'well I'm sorry you don't trust me, Roger.'

'But I do, dear boy… it's the bloody Chinese murderer I don't trust!'

I gave a nod, and asked, 'do you ever intend to come back?'

'Probably not… I've had enough of life here, and need a big change before I get any older.'

'…A midlife crisis then?'

'Probably… but, I'll see a new life with Leisha… and, that I can promise!'

'I'm sure you can… and, you'll probably soon be dead from over exertion…'

'Ah, what a bloody good way to go!' he replied, with a broad smile.

'…So, what about your career?'

He shrugged his shoulders, and replied, 'bollocks to all that… I've had more than enough of crooks… never mind the bloody clients in the dock!' I had to smile at his description of his colleagues, and thought, 'how very true.'

During the meal he talked lovingly about Leisha, and the life they planned together… and, I wondered if he was building castles in the air. I tried several times to persuade him to reconsider what he was doing, but it was to no avail… and, I had to face the real possibility that I might never see my friend again.

It was with sadness that we shook hands, and said our final 'goodbyes' outside the restaurant. I climbed into the Bentley and drove home with a heavy heart.

CHAPTER 11

WILL IT NEVER END?

It was just after one o'clock the next day, we having lunch in the kitchen, when the phone rang.
'Hello.'
'Mr Cavendish, I'm now safely back in London,' said Lu Ming.
'Ah, that's good to know, sir... and, are you alright?'
'Yes I am, thank you... now, I'd like you to come to see me, so I can reward you for the flight to France, and everything you did for me in Switzerland.'
'That will be a pleasure, sir,' I replied, thinking that I might, hopefully, receive another fifty thousand pounds.
'Good... shall we say sometime this evening, if that's convenient for you?'
'Yes it is, sir, I can be with you by about seven.'
'Excellent... my wife and I look forward to seeing you then... goodbye, Mr Cavendish.'
'Goodbye, sir,' I replied, while thinking that Leisha was obviously still with him, and wondering if Lu Ming knew about Roger.

The drive up to London was effortless in the Bentley, and I went straight to Grosvenor Square. I assumed that now the authorities had Lu Ming entrapped in the legal system, it didn't matter if the Americans or the police saw me arrive at his home.
The smiling Chinese maid opened the door, welcomed me politely and immediately showed me into the study, where Lu Ming stood up from his desk.
'Ah, Mr Cavendish... I'm happy to see you again... please be seated,' he said, with a smile, as he waved me to sit.
'Thank you, sir.'
'I've had a few adventures since we last met,' he said, as he resumed his seat.
'So I believe.'

'Oh yes indeed... the Swiss police and their judiciary are not the easiest of people to deal with,' he said, with a sigh.

'I'm sure of that, sir.'

'... And, I want to thank you, and the little French girl, for all you did to help me in Zürich.'

'It was the least we could do.'

'Well, it is much appreciated Mr Cavendish... now, to recompense you for the flight and all your troubles, I have in this briefcase seventy five thousand pounds ... and, I hope you will give the French girl a little reward,' he said, with a smile, as he produced a black briefcase from under his desk. He placed it on the desk, before clicking it open to reveal the cash in neat bundles.

I was taken aback by the enormous sum, for a moment, before saying, 'this is extremely generous of you, sir.'

'Not at all, it's my duty to reward you for your help, in difficult circumstances... besides, I'm a wealthy man and can afford it.'

'Well, thank you, sir... and, I will see that Hélène is rewarded.'

'Good,' he said, with a smile... and, at that moment, I heard the door behind me open, and close.

'Ah, Leisha, my dear... come and say 'hello' to Mr Cavendish... my saviour!'

I turned to see Leisha, looking gorgeous in a shimmering, red satin evening dress, with a halter neckline... so tightly fitting, it looked as if she had been poured into it!

Leisha smiled as she crossed the room, and held out her hand, saying, 'good evening, Mr Cavendish... or may I call you Peter?'

'...Of course.'

'It's so nice to see you again.'

'... And you too, Mrs Ming,' I replied, as I caught a whiff of her perfume.

'Oh, please call me Leisha... everyone does!'

'You're very kind,' I replied, with a smile.

'So, when you've finished your business with my husband, Peter, won't you come through for some food and drinks?'

'That will be very pleasant, thank you.'

'Good... now, this is for you, dear,' she said to Lu Ming, as she bent over and placed an envelope on the desk, beside the briefcase.

The sight of her beautiful, pert bottom, tightly encased in

shimmering red satin, conjured up a picture in my mind of her firing ping pong balls, from that position, whilst naked... and, I suddenly became very hot under the collar! I realised why my friend could not possibly resist this glamorous, sexy woman who could perform such wonderful tricks... and, who could?

Leisha left us to talk for a while, and Lu Ming told me, in detail, about all his troubles in Zürich. As he spoke, I wondered *'if he intends to murder his wife, and then kill me, why would he give me the cash? Surely he would have made some excuse to not pay me if he planned to kill me, or perhaps he wanted to just lull me into a false sense of security...'* I was now thoroughly confused by it all.

Eventually, Lu Ming finished his diatribe of misery in Zürich, and led the way into the dining room, where Leisha had laid out a feast, with enough food for a Chinese Emperor. As we chatted, I enjoyed the delicious food, while noticing that Leisha was very loving towards her husband... there was no sign of any disharmony between them. Obviously Leisha had no intentions of leaving her rich husband for an out-of-work barrister! It was ever thus... with money being the greatest aphrodisiac!

As I prepared to leave, Lu Ming said he would be in touch within a few days, as he had another little job for me. I was quite happy, if it carried a substantial cash fee... and, told him so. He and Leisha smiled, we shook hands, and I took the briefcase from him in the hallway, before we all said 'goodbye.'

As I slipped behind the wheel of the Bentley, my phone rang.
  'Hello.'
  'Peter its Roger....'
  'Well, hello there... I didn't think I'd be hearing from you ever again!'
  'I know... I know...'
  'So, where are you now?'
  'At Heathrow...'
  '...Heathrow?'
  'Yes... I'm still waiting for Leisha... do you know where she is?'

'Yes… she's at home with her husband…'

'Oh Fuck!'

'Precisely… so, what are you going to do now?'

'I really don't know… she was supposed to meet me at terminal 5, at midday!'

I glanced at the dashboard clock and said, 'well it's now half past eight, so I presume you've missed the flight to your 'secret wherever destination.'

'Yes, we bloody well have!'

'Well, some women are so unpredictable… and, sadly you've just found one who's stood you up!'

'Tell me about it!'

'So, what are you planning to do now?'

Roger sighed, and replied, 'I suppose I'll have to book into a hotel, and think about what I'm going to do next.'

'Well, keep in touch and let me know.'

He sighed again, and replied, 'I will… bye, Peter.'

As I started the Bentley, I thought this situation was entirely predictable, and Roger had only himself to blame. After a few more moments of deliberation, I made my way out of London, to join the Motorway… which would take me home to Louise and the babes.

Arriving back at the farm in the early hours, I told a sleepy, but curious, Louise what had happened in London, and about Roger's call… she laughed before falling asleep.

I enjoyed two days of peace, whilst attending to various jobs that needed to be done around the farm. Bob and the boys were always enthusiastic, and were good to be with, as there was lots of leg pulling and laughs. It was just after eight in the evening, on the second day, that the phone rang. I thought it might be Lu Ming, or possibly Roger… it was Lu Ming.

'Mr Cavendish, can you come to London tonight?'

'Well, it's a bit late now…'

'It's a very urgent matter… so, please be here as soon as you can,' he said, sounding desperate.

I thought of the money, every man has his price, and replied, 'alright, I'll leave now, and be with you as soon as...'

'Thank you, Mr Cavendish.'

I returned to the kitchen, and told Louise.

'I hope you aren't getting in any deeper with this man,' she said, firmly.

'Well, I'll try to keep my distance.'

'Good... and, see that you do!'

'I will... promise.'

'... And, I don't expect you'll be home until the early hours again,' she said, with a resigned sigh.

'Probably not... so, sleep tight, darling.'

'I will... if the babes don't wake me!'

As I cruised effortlessly up to London, I wondered what Lu Ming wanted, that was so urgent. I would soon know, and prepared myself mentally for something unpleasant... and, I was not wrong. The maid opened the door, and this time she wasn't smiling. Without a word, she ushered me into his study, where he stood up from his desk, looking pale.

'I'm so glad you've come,' he said in a whisper.

'So, what do you want me for?'

'There's been a terrible accident... it's Leisha...' he replied haltingly, and I guessed she was dead.

'What's happened to your wife, and where is she now?'

'Upstairs on her bed... would you like to see her?'

'I presume she's dead?'

'Unfortunately she is... it was an accident, Mr Cavendish... a dreadful accident,' he replied, but I didn't believe him... not for one moment. Had he found out about Roger and Leisha? Was my friend the next on this Chinaman's death list... and would my death follow?

The questions cascaded through my mind, before I said, 'yes I'd like to see your wife, sir.'

He nodded, and replied, 'please come with me.'

I followed him out of the study, up the ornate marble staircase, and then into a large bedroom, off the plush, carpeted corridor. Leisha lay on the bed, dressed in exotic black lace underwear, looking as if she were asleep... but when I touched her lovely face, it was stone cold, and I wondered how long she had been dead.

I turned to face him, and asked, 'so what happened?'

'She fell, quite accidently, down the stairs... and, I think she's broken her neck,' he replied... but, I knew he was lying.

'Why didn't you call an ambulance?'

'I wasn't here... the maid found her,' he replied.

'...So, where you, sir?'

'I'd gone for a long walk in Hyde Park, to try and think... then, when I returned, I found Leisha on the stairs... and, she was obviously dead,' he said, as he began to cry. I couldn't decide whether he was a very good actor, or genuinely upset.

'Why didn't you call the police?'

'I didn't know what to do... I was in a panic,' he replied, between gentle sobs.

'I'm sure you were... so, when did this all happen?'

'This afternoon,' he whispered.

I nodded, and turned back to look at the beauty... and, knew he would ask me to dispose of her. There followed a few minutes of silence, before he asked, 'so, Mr Cavendish... will you take care of her?'

'I'm not sure I can, sir.'

'...Why not?'

'Because I think you should inform the police,' I replied firmly.

'I can't do that!'

'...Why not?'

'You know why not!'

'Do I?'

'Mr Cavendish... you know that I am in a very difficult situation with the authorities in Switzerland, America, and here in Britain... so, this tragic accident will raise doubts about me that will probably cause further unwanted investigations into my affairs!'

'Well, if it was an accident, I think you've nothing to fear, sir.'

He looked angry, and then asked, 'do you really think that I murdered my lovely wife?'

'It's a possibility.'

'But why should I do that?'

'I really don't know, sir... only you can answer that.'

He shook his head, and then sat in a chair next to the bed. He put his head in his hands and began to cry once more.

I was moved by this outpouring of grief, and when he whispered, 'my life is now over without my Leisha,' it confirmed to me that he was genuine. I felt pity for this generous man and, against all my inclinations, said quietly, 'alright, I'll take care of her for you, sir.' He looked up, smiled and said, 'oh thank you, thank you so much... you have relieved me of a great personal burden, Mr Cavendish.'

I just nodded and asked, 'so, I presume you'll say that she has returned to China?'

'Yes, of course I will... and, no one will ever know the terrible truth.'

'No indeed... now, is there a back entrance here?' I asked, thinking about the CCTV cameras at the American Embassy.

'Yes, there is... it leads to a narrow alleyway, where some residents park their cars.'

'Right, let me wrap her in a blanket, and I'll carry her down.'

He nodded, produced a blue blanket from a chest of drawers, and gave it to me... but, before I could wrap Leisha's cold body in the blanket, he gently kissed her forehead, and said something in Cantonese, while gazing at her lovely face. I gave him a moment to compose himself, before I placed the blanket around her lifeless body, and lifted her from the bed. I followed Lu Ming out of the bedroom and down the stairs to the back door, where I laid the body.

'I'll get my car and bring it around,' I said, and he nodded.

I tried to look relaxed climbing into the Bentley, as I was sure the cameras would see me, and dove slowly out of the square, before driving around the block, looking for the entrance to the alleyway... which I hoped was out of the range of the CCTV cameras. I found it with some difficulty, and drove slowly along the alleyway, only to have my progress blocked by a large white Mercedes. There's always one, isn't there? I cursed, slipped from the Bentley and made my way along to a gate in the high wall, behind the house, from where Lu Ming suddenly appeared and waved. I followed him into the house, picked up Leisha, hurried back to the Bentley and placed her lifeless body in the cavernous boot.

After closing the boot, I looked at his pale face, and said, 'I'll be in touch, sir.'

'Yes... and, thank you Mr Cavendish... I will reward you well for this kindness.'

I nodded, then slipped behind the wheel, and slowly reversed out of the alleyway.

I drove away from the square with my heart thumping, wondering why I was doing this dreadful thing once again. I was sure my actions, which started by helping Roger, would haunt me for the rest of my life... and, it depressed me. I drove carefully, while watching my speed through London, and only allowed the Bentley to speed up on the Motorway. The nearer I got to the farm, the more relaxed I became, and reasoned that only two hours flying would see the mission completed... never to be repeated!

As I pulled into the yard, dawn was breaking. I glanced at the dashboard clock, it was just after four, so I would be back by six... hopefully Bob and the boys wouldn't be about by then. After driving down to the aircraft and placing Leisha in the passenger seat, I left the Bentley parked nearby. I quickly carried out the cockpit checks, and then to my horror, I noticed that the two fuel gauges read just less than half-full, which meant I, probably, had only two hours flying at cruise speed.

So, to be safe, I would only fly for forty five minutes, out over the Atlantic, to dispose of Leisha. I started up, checked the magnetos, engine pressures and temperature, before releasing the brake and giving full throttle to the engine. Papa Oscar lifted from the strip with ease and I climbed to a thousand feet and headed out across Lyme Bay, to the grey, rolling Atlantic beyond.

The flight settled down, after I had selected seventy five per cent throttle, and the air speed reached one hundred knots... so, there was nothing for me to do now, except watch the time. I checked the compass heading of two three zero, and only occasionally adjusted it by using slight rudder corrections. As it grew lighter, the sea below took on a lovely blue tinge, with little flecks of white where the rolling waves broke. I felt very sad that I would soon commit the body of this lovely woman to the cold unforgiving sea. I wondered if I should tell Roger that Leisha was dead, or that she had returned to China... neither was a good option, as I knew he would be totally devastated... but, if he thought she was alive, he might hope that she would return, or, worst of all, he would go and search for her... perish that thought! It was a true and vexing dilemma for me and I didn't know the best way forward.

If I told Roger the truth, he might be able to accept it as time passed, although the loss of a deeply loved one never fades... and, the emotional scars and memories remain for ever. After some deep contemplation for a time, I decided to tell my friend the truth, and felt much better for my decision. I glanced at my watch, I had now been flying for half an hour, so only another fifteen minutes to go before I said 'goodbye' to Leisha. The minutes passed agonisingly slowly, but when the time had elapsed, I drew a deep breath, banked Papa Oscar over to sixty degrees, opened the passenger door and, after one final admiring glance at Leisha, pushed her lifeless body out. I watched it tumble down to the waves below, where it disappeared with barely a splash. Tears were coursing down my cheeks, as I turned the aircraft around to the reciprocal compass heading, which would take me back to the strip.

As I crossed the coastline, the engine fluttered for a moment, I glanced at the fuel gauges and my blood ran cold! The needles were firmly stuck on empty, so had I miscalculated my fuel use... and thought, 'now what?'

A forced landing in some field would cause problems! The CAA would investigate the flight, after all the emergency services would have to attend... dear God, what a mess! I decided to try and glide back to the strip, and prayed that I would make it... and not crash! I eased the throttle back to conserve what fuel was left, and lowered the nose slightly to maintain air speed. The engine spluttered again and my heart raced, I glanced at the air speed, noted it had reduced to eighty knots, and I knew that I would soon have to pick a field for a forced landing.

I aged years at every splutter and short-lived engine recovery, but as the farm came slowly into view, I felt that I might yet make it back safely. I lowered the nose slightly, checked the airspeed, which was now down to seventy knots, and tightened my straps… just in case I ended up in an adjacent field, full of my neighbour's cows. My house now loomed larger as the engine finally stopped, and knew I had only one chance to land, there would be no 'going around' if I missed! I made a tight circuit while checking the speed, lined up with the strip, passed over the house by about ten feet, let the speed decay to fifty knots, flared and landed heavily… I then slammed on the brakes, to stop Papa Oscar over shooting into the hedge at the end. When the aircraft had stopped and everything was completely silent, I breathed a sigh of relief, and noticed my hands were shaking. I knew I couldn't do this ever again, and my days of disposing of bodies out in the Atlantic were now over. After a few minutes sitting quietly to compose myself, I switched off all the systems and clambered down from the cockpit.

The fresh smell of the morning engulfed me as I strode up towards the house, and it was good to have survived once again. As I got nearer to the house, I noticed two men standing by a black Range Rover… I recognised them with horror! I glanced casually at my awkwardly parked Bentley as they stepped forward to meet me, before I called out wearily, 'hello, gentlemen, what can I do to help you today?'

'Hi, Mr Cavendish… would you mind telling us where you've taken Lu Ming?' asked Harwood in a firm tone.

'I don't know what you're talking about,' I replied as I reached them.

'Well, we guess where ever you've flown him to… it's was a damned long way, because you've just managed to land right out of fuel!'

'That was a miscalculation on my part, gentlemen,' I said with a smile.

'Lucky you made it back then.'

'Indeed, but I'm used to dramas in flying.'

'Huh, maybe... so, where have you taken him?'

'I haven't taken Lu Ming anywhere...'

'We know you were at his house last night...'

'So?'

'Mr Cavendish, you're in a very difficult position, and unless you start helping us, you'll be in a world of trouble!' said Cooper.

'...Oh, really?' I asked sarcastically.

Harwood glared at me and said, 'Yes... after you left Lu Ming last night, we called at the house and he'd disappeared... so, it's probable that you sneaked him out the back way, and brought him here... and, after unloading his luggage in a God-damned hurry, from your parked there,' he pointed at the Bentley... 'then flew him someplace... so, where to, Mr Cavendish?'

If only they knew what I really had done!

I decided to go on the attack and asked, 'have you spoken to Mrs Lu Ming about her husband's whereabouts?'

'She wasn't there... and, the place is empty,' replied Harwood.

'Well, she was last night,' I said truthfully, and almost added, 'but unfortunately dead!'

'So, perhaps you've flown them both out of here!'

'That's a possibility, but absolutely not true... because I went for an early flight on my own, for relaxation... as I often do!'

At that moment Bob arrived, looked at the Americans, and asked, 'everything okay, boss?'

'Yes, thanks, Bob, I'll chat inside with these gentlemen, over a coffee,' I replied, with a smile.

'Right,' said Bob, as the boys arrived.

The Americans followed me into the kitchen, where Louise stood holding Samantha, who was crying, while Scott was sitting at the table, grizzling. Louise was in her dressing gown and looked as if she had been dragged through a hedge backwards... she said, angrily, 'ah, there you are at last... I've not had a good night!'

'Neither have I!'

The following Americans gazed at Louise, before she asked, 'I don't supposed either of you are good with children?' They shook their heads, and smiled. Once we were out in the hallway, I heard her shout, 'and I suppose you'll want some coffee?'

'Please,' I replied, as I led them into the study.

Once they were seated, I said firmly, 'you've had another wasted journey, gentlemen, because I haven't the faintest idea where Lu Ming, or his wife are... so, after you have had your coffee, I think you best leave and try to find out... and, how they've given you the slip!'

That hurt them, Harwood sighed and replied, 'Mr Cavendish, we damn well know that you are mixed up with this man somehow, and it's in your best interest to help us.'

'Mr Harwood, you're hopelessly wrong... I know nothing... nothing at all about his business or current whereabouts...'

'You flew him to France recently!' interrupted Cooper.

'Indeed, I did... but, that doesn't mean I know where he is now!'

'So, what the hell were you doing at his house last night?' asked Harwood.

'It was really a social occasion, his wife likes me... which is understandable... but, he did talk about a job for me, in a few days,' I replied.

'What sort of job?'

'He didn't go into any detail, but I assumed he wanted me to fly him somewhere,' I replied, as Louise arrived with the coffees. They thanked her, as Louise gave me a quizzical look and left... so, I knew I would have to tell her everything about last night's adventures.

Over coffee, the conversation went around in circles, before they had endured enough and decided to leave. I wished them a safe journey back to London, and Harwood responded that they would return for sure. I just smiled, followed them out to their Range Rover, and gave them a fond wave farewell as they drove off.

I went back to the kitchen, where Louise stood, with her hands on her hips, and asked, 'well?'

That single word holds a myriad of questions, that must be answered, but I replied, 'this morning I landed with no fuel!'

'…Oh God!'

'…And it was touch and go whether I would get back safely… so, before I tell you everything, I'm driving over to the club to get some fuel!'

My wife was strangely speechless for once!

I strode out to the Bentley and drove over to the club, for some aviation fuel.

I found Jimmy refuelling a Cherokee, and when he'd finished, he went in search of a twenty five litre container, which he then filled with fuel. I returned to the farm, and was pleased that Bob and the boys had pushed Papa Oscar back up to the house. The Cessna was quickly refuelled, with enough to allow me to fly back to the club to fill the tanks. I ran the engine on 'tick over' for a while, to ensure no muck had ended up in the carburettor. When I was satisfied everything was okay, I took off and, after landing at the club, Papa Oscar was fully refuelled.

Over a leisurely breakfast, I told Louise everything, and other than her gasps of surprise at the appropriate moments, she said nothing until I had finished, then asked, 'so what are you going to do now?'

'Go to bed, I've been up all night…'

'So have I.'

'… And then I'll have to tell Roger that Leisha is dead,' I said, which I did not relish!

CHAPTER 12

IT ALL GETS VERY DIFFICULT BEFORE THE END

After resting all that afternoon, followed by a good night's sleep, I felt much better the next morning, and I was ready for the day ahead. Over a full breakfast, I talked to Louise about Roger, and she agreed that it was likely that he would do something drastic to Lu Ming or himself, after I told him that Leisha was dead.

'…And, he mustn't come here looking for her grave,' said Louise.

'No, of course not… and, if he ever found out I'd disposed of her far out in the Atlantic, he'd go absolutely mad!'

'He would… so, what do you propose to do next?'

'I think I'll fly up to Kidlington, see Paula and ask for her advice, before I call Roger and find out where he is.'

'Good thinking, darling.'

I kissed my understanding wife and went to the study, where I phoned my voluptuous aunt to ask if she was free to see me today.

'Of course, darling… come for lunch… it won't be much, but I'll rustle up something!' said Paula.

'Thanks… I'll be with you at about midday.'

'…Lovely… looking forward to it… bye.'

I thought that if the Americans, or Scotland Yard, were tapping my phone, they would think I was only on a social visit to Paula… which suited me nicely, as there is nothing so innocent as a man, with nothing to hide, visiting his aunt for lunch!

I flew up to Kidlington feeling very relaxed, but found myself constantly glancing at the fuel gauges! I suppose I needed some reassurance after my recent adventure, but all was well, and I landed just before midday at the busy little airport. A taxi drove me out to Yarnton, where Paula greeted me with a big, lingering kiss, while she hugged me so close that I could feel her breasts pushing hard into me. She is always very sexual and suggestive!

'So, tell me all your news, darling,' she said, as she led me to the kitchen and clicked the kettle on. I sat at the table, and replied, 'well, I've lots to tell you and need your advice.'

'Well, this sounds interesting... tea or coffee?'

'...Coffee, please.'

'Right... so, do go on.'

I took a deep breath, and said, 'I'm afraid that Leisha is dead, and I have disposed of her body...'

Paula whirled around, and asked in astonishment, 'Leisha is dead?'

'Yes...'

'Dear God... was she murdered?'

'I don't think so...'

'Then how did she die?'

'Lu Ming said it was an accident... she fell down the stairs and broke her neck.'

'... And, do you believe that?'

'Well...' and was going on to say, 'I do,' but paused momentarily.

'You're hesitating, darling... that means you have doubts!' she interrupted, before pouring the water into the coffee cups. I smiled and replied, 'Paula, you're right as usual. I thought, at the time, it seemed plausible, because Lu Ming said he was out of the house when it happened... according to him, the maid found her, and when he returned, he panicked... he didn't call the authorities, but phoned me, and I drove up to London.'

'... And, now you've had second thoughts?'

'Yes, I think I have.'

'So, what do you think really happened?'

'Well, I don't know for sure, but perhaps he found out about her affair with Roger...'

'Surely he wouldn't murder her for that!' she interrupted.

'Some men are very jealous and capable of anything.'

'Oh, yes... indeed they are!'

'Besides, if what Natasha told me is true about Leisha, taking millions from his bank in Hong Kong, then he could have easily done it.'

'Now, that is a motive I can understand,' said Paula, with a smile.

'You're ever the business woman,' I said.

She gave a mischievous grin, and replied, 'it always comes down to either sex or money, darling!'

'True… and now, I have to tell Roger that his mistress, who did such fascinating things with her body, is dead.'

'Yes, I'm afraid you do.'

'… And, he will never forgive himself for not running away with her after they first met.'

'Possibly… but, you must tell him that he couldn't have known what was to happen.'

'Of course I will, but that doesn't make it any easier for him.'

Paula sighed and sipped her coffee, before asking, 'so, when are you going to tell him?'

'I don't know… and, I don't even know where he is at the moment,' I replied.

'Well, I think you should take him somewhere quiet when you do.'

'Yes, I will… and, I am concerned that he might do something foolish…'

'Like commit suicide?' she interrupted.

'Yes… or probably murder!'

'…Lu Ming?'

'Of course… and, Roger will automatically think that he killed her because of their affair.'

'Oh, what a mess,' she whispered.

'It is… and, I dread telling him that Leisha is dead.'

'I'm sure you do… so, let's have some lunch, while I try and think this through.'

Over a delicious mushroom omelette and chips, we talked about Roger, but came to no firm conclusions. After lunch, we went into the drawing room, and Paula had just started giving her advice, on how I should tell him the grim news, when my phone rang.

'I bet that's Roger,' she said, with a smile… and it was!

I smiled at her, as I said, 'hello.'

'Peter… it's Roger.'

'How are you, Roger?' I asked, and nodded at Paula.

'Okay, I think.'

'…And, where are you?'

'I'm staying at the Randolph, in Oxford, at the moment... I've been out to Witney several times, looking for Leisha, but she's not there.'

'I'm truly sorry for you, Roger.'

'Thanks... you don't happen to know where she is, do you?'

'No, Roger, I don't,' I replied truthfully.

'Pity... well, I'll just have to keep on looking for her...'

'Roger, listen... I'm with Paula at the moment, so I'm close to you, and I think it would be a good idea if we could meet at the Randolph,' I interrupted.

'Oh, it would be bloody good to see you, Peter... I need to talk, so come when you're ready.'

'Right... I'll see you soon... bye.'

'Bye, Peter.'

I glanced at Paula, who said, 'and now you're about to tell your best friend a terrible truth.'

I sighed, nodded, and said, 'yes, I am.'

'Well, be gentle with him, darling.'

'I'll try.'

'Take my car, and stay with him as long as you like.'

'Thanks, Paula,' I said, then leaned over and gave her a kiss on her cheek.

I drove to Oxford as quickly as I dare, and parked in the hotel car park, before hurrying to reception, from where I phoned Roger, and then went up to his room. I knocked, he opened the door and tried to smile, but he looked dreadful.

'It's good to see you, Peter,' he said, as I entered the room.

'So, how are you really?' I asked before sitting in a chair by the window.

'Okay... I suppose,' he replied hesitantly, as he sank down on the bed, opposite me.

'How long are you staying here?'

He sighed, and replied, 'just another night, then I thought I'd go back to London and see if she's there.'

This was the moment to tell him the dreadful truth, but I hesitated then he looked at me quizzically, and asked, 'you bloody well know what's happened to her, don't you?'

I nodded and replied, 'yes, I do, Roger.'

'Well?' he asked.

There is that word again that demands a myriad of answers!

'I'm afraid that Leisha is dead...'

'Oh dear God, no... not my Leisha... not my lovely Leisha!' he exclaimed, before bursting into tears. I sat next to him on the bed, put my arm around him, and said gently, 'it's true... and, I'm so very sorry for you.'

'Oh God, Peter, what am I to do?'

'I don't know for the moment, but you have to face the fact that you'll never see her again.'

'I can't believe it... how did she die?'

'It was a terrible accident... she fell down the stairs and broke her neck...'

'Where was this?' he interrupted.

'...At her home, in London.'

'Well, her bloody murderous husband probably killed her!'

'Why?' I asked, expecting him to say, 'he found out about our affair,' but he replied, 'because of the maid and the money!'

'...The maid and the money?'

'Yes, Leisha told me that you disposed of her...'

'I did, but why would Lu Ming murder Leisha over that?'

'Because the maid was actually Lu Ming's niece... it seems he was very fond of her... a bit too fond, according to Leisha, and she hated the girl... so, I think she murdered the niece and blamed it on Lu's mother!'

His reply shocked me, and I asked, 'so why did Leisha hate her?'

'...Because the niece was always spying on her, and then telling Lu.'

'My God,' I whispered, then asked, 'and what about the money?'

'Leisha told me that she had managed to drain all the money from Lu Ming's bank accounts in Hong Kong, and had transferred the money to Switzerland... and, we were going to live nicely on that, after she left him.'

I sighed, finding it all hard to believe, and said, 'well that can't happen now, Roger.'

'I know… I know,' he slowly whispered, and I felt sorry for my friend.

'So, what do you plan to do next?'

'I haven't a bloody clue… but, I'd like to see Lu Ming, and hear what he has to say about Leisha's accident… before I murder him!'

'Roger… I realise you're deeply upset, but you really mustn't do anything stupid.'

He didn't answer, and I could almost see the wheels in his brain ticking over… he was confused… and who wouldn't be, under the circumstances?

After a few moments he looked at me, and asked, 'is she buried on the farm?'

I took a deep breath and replied gently, 'Roger, it's best that you don't know where she is, but I promise you that she is dead.'

He nodded, and said, 'you're probably right… has anybody told her sister?'

'…Her sister?'

'Yes, she's two years younger than Leisha, and she lives in Hong Kong… her name is Tai Lu… I think they were very close.'

'…Really?'

'Yes, so has anybody told her?'

'I don't know, but I expect Lu Ming will tell her,' I replied

'I wouldn't be so sure… that man is a real bastard, and only cares about himself and his money!'

'That I can believe… so, will you tell the sister?' I asked… he waited for a moment, and then said, 'I think I'll fly out and see Tai Lu… much better that way, and it'll give me time to think.'

'Do you think that's sensible?'

'Yes, I do… and, somebody's got to do it!' he replied, and I worried about my friend, travelling alone to Hong Kong.

'Well, before you book your ticket, just pause and think for a moment.'

'There's nothing to think about, Peter… so, I'm going,' he said firmly.

I thought, 'dear God, there's nothing like an obstinate man, who won't listen to reason!' and asked, 'why don't you come and stay at the farm, for a while?'

'No thanks.'

'It'll give you some time to think, Roger… and, you need that just now.'

'I said no thanks… I'll sort myself out, if you don't mind!'

'Then, be my guest… I'm only trying to help, but you seem to be beyond my help at the moment.'

'Yes, I am… so, I think you'd better go now, Peter… I'll be in touch.'

'…Promise?'

'Yes I promise,' he hissed, in an agitated tone.

'Okay… and, I'm just a phone call away, if you need me.'

'I know, I know,' he whispered, and gave a nod of his head.

'Bye, Roger,' I said, as I stood up and made for the door.

'Bye, old chap.'

As I drove away from the hotel, I wondered if I would ever see him again. I thought it very unlikely, if he went to Hong Kong in search of Tai Lu, especially if she was as provocative with ping pong balls as Leisha!

Over a cup of tea, I told Paula everything, and she wasn't surprised at Roger's behaviour… saying that she didn't think that if he went to Hong Kong, he would ever return.

A little later, Paula drove me out to the airport where I said 'goodbye' to my aunt, before she gave me a long, lingering, wet kiss… she's a devil of a temptress, don't you think?

I flew back to the farm, with many thoughts cascading through my mind… but, landed safely, after checking my fuel gauges!

Over dinner, I told Louise what had transpired, and she agreed with Paula, that if Roger went to Hong Kong, we would never see him again. With that thought in mind, I began to feel quite relaxed, but I would certainly miss my good old school friend. Unfortunately, he was the architect of his disasters, and had dragged me into a maelstrom of events, that I never wanted to repeat! Life would now be much quieter without Roger… how wrong I was!

Two days later Lu Ming phoned.
'Mr Cavendish… I'd like to see you tomorrow, if you're free.'
'Yes I am,' I replied, thinking of the money he owed me for the disposal of his wife.
'Good, I'm staying at the Savoy, in London… please meet me there at three tomorrow.'
'I'll be there, sir.'
'Thank you… I look forward to seeing you… goodbye.'
'Goodbye, sir.'

After I told Louise, she was anxious about me seeing the Chinese businessman again.
'I think he only wants to pay me, darling,' I said, with a smile.
'But you don't know that!' she retorted, sharply.
'No, but I'm sure I'm probably right.'
'Hmm… we'll have to wait and see then, won't we?'

It was just before ten o'clock when I set off in the Bentley, for London. After a smooth drive, I parked at Marble Arch, as usual, took the underground to Charing Cross, and walked up the Strand, to the Savoy. Lu Ming was waiting in reception; he stood and smiled when I entered.
'Good afternoon, Mr Cavendish.'
'Good afternoon, sir.'
'I'm so pleased that you came… shall we go into the lounge and have some tea?'
'Yes, that would be very pleasant, sir,' I replied, with a smile.
At first, he led the way through, but then slowed so he was alongside me, and whispered, 'where is your car?'
'At Marble Arch, in the underground car park.'
'Good… after you leave me, wait in your car and I will be with you in an hour.'
'Right,' I replied, knowing that we were being watched.

We sat in comfortable seats in the corner, with a small table in front of us. Lu Ming raised his hand and caught a waiter's eye, who hurried over and took the order for our tea. After he had left us, Lu Ming started telling me about his early life in Beijing, and he droned on until the tea arrived. He only stopped talking to sip his tea, and I wondered what was coming next. Then came the surprise!

'Mr Cavendish, I was married twice before I met Leisha, and if anything untoward happens to me, I want you to go to Beijing and tell my ex-wives… here are their names and addresses,' he said, as he produced a folded piece of paper from his inside jacket pocket, and handed it to me.

I was stunned and momentarily speechless, before asking, 'do you think that you're in any danger, sir?'

'It's a strong possibility.'

'…From whom?'

He sighed, and replied, 'as I told you previously, a number of factions want me dead, Mr Cavendish…principally, the Chinese Government.'

'Well far be it from me to ask 'why', sir.'

'Quite, and let's leave it that way… now, I have a number of urgent things to attend too, so I'll leave you, Mr Cavendish… and thank you for coming.' With that, he smiled, stood up and hurried from the lounge.

I left the Savoy, retraced my steps to Marble Arch and sat in the Bentley, awaiting Lu Ming's arrival. I spent the next hour contemplating what it was all about, and hoped that I wasn't in any danger! I looked at the paper with his ex-wives names and addresses on, and wondered if I would ever have to go to Beijing. Only time would tell. Suddenly, he appeared from the pedestrian entrance, which leads down from Park Lane. He was carrying a briefcase, which I hoped contained my money, and a leather holdall. I slipped from the car and waved to him… he smiled, and hurried towards me. After placing the luggage on the back seat, we sat in front.

'Well, Mr Cavendish, I'm sure you're wondering what this is all about.'

'I am, sir.'

'Let me start by saying that I am now under constant

surveillance.'

'I'm certain that you are, sir.'

'However, I trust you implicitly…'

'Thank you, sir.'

'… And, I know that what I am about to tell you will remain confidential for ever.'

I didn't much care for the 'for ever' bit, but just nodded in agreement.

'I have kept up some pretence before deciding that you are a man who could be trusted with my life.'

'I'm pleased that you hold me in such high regard, sir,' I said, hoping he'd give me my money and leave, but he didn't!

'I do… and now, the truth… I hated my wife… she was a violent, unscrupulous, vindictive, immoral woman, of the very worst kind!'

That surprised me, as he continued, 'she managed to transfer millions of pounds from my business accounts in Hong Kong to a Swiss bank, in Zürich…' I thought, 'so Natasha was right!'

Lu Ming continued, 'fortunately the chief executive of my bank informed me of the transfer, so I was able to trace the money.'

'That was very fortunate, sir.'

'Yes… and, she planned to divorce me and live on my money with her latest lover, somewhere in secret… but, I would have found them, and dealt with them in my own fashion!' This made me shiver, as I realised how close Roger had come!

'Do you know who this man is, sir?'

'No, but I will find out in due course,' he replied, and I shivered again.

'So, can I help you in any way, sir?' I asked lamely.

'Oh yes, I have plans for you, Mr Cavendish… well rewarded plans… and, this is what I want you to do…' he replied, and suddenly I became very anxious.

He continued, 'I want to stay with you, at your farm tonight…' I was horrified, and Louise would have a fit!

'…And, in the morning I want you to fly me to Besancon again, and ask the pretty French girl…'

'Hélène,' I interrupted helpfully.

'Yes, Hélène … to drive us to Zürich… so I can retrieve my

money from the bank, and return to your farm… then you can drive me to my house, in Witney.'

My mind was a whirl of questions, and I asked, 'so, how will you bring all the money back, sir?'

'It will be in bearer bonds, of one hundred thousand pounds each…. So, it will all fit into a briefcase,' he replied.

'May I ask how much money there is in the bank, sir?'

'Yes, you may… it is over six million pounds… I want you to hide it on your farm… you're good at hiding things!' he replied, and I was speechless!

He looked at me, and said, 'you've gone quite pale, Mr Cavendish… are you alright?'

'Yes, yes, I think so, sir… it's all just come as a bit of a shock.'

'Yes, I'm sure… now, can we drive to your farm?' he asked, I just nodded and he added, 'we can talk on the way.' I started the Bentley with my mind now in a constant state of nervous worry!

Once on the Motorway, my nerves settled down, and I decided to ask him some awkward questions, about Leisha.

'As you are now trusting me implicitly, sir… I'd like to know if you murdered your wife.'

'No, Mr Cavendish, I didn't… it was a terrible accident, but the truth is that we did have a violent argument in our bedroom, which carried on out to the landing where, regrettably, I pushed her, she fell backwards, then down the stairs. I went down to the bottom of the stairs and felt her pulse, but she was obviously dead. The maid heard the row and came to look… I told her that my wife had fainted and would be alright, and then I carried her up to the bedroom, and went out to think. I decided that her death would be too difficult to explain in my present circumstances, and I was concerned that it would go badly for me, so after I returned, I called you.'

'Hmm… I see.'

'…And, the reason for this latest row was because of the letter she gave me when you were with me,' he said.

'May I ask what it said?'

'Yes… she told me that she was getting a divorce, to be with someone else… and, I told her to forget such nonsense!'

'Did you know anything about her lover?'

'No, only that he was the latest in a long line of men... fascinated by her beauty and the sexual tricks she could do,' he replied.

'I see.'

'...And, I wonder if you do, Mr Cavendish... I've already told you that my wife was an unscrupulous, violent woman.'

'Yes, you have, sir.'

'She murdered my niece, you know, and blamed my mother... then asked you to dispose of her... I was heartbroken, but played along, knowing I would eventually avenge her,' he said, and I wondered what was really true... perhaps I would never know. I decided that I had heard enough for now, and concentrated on the logistics of getting him to Zürich and back. I had recently bought a new mobile phone with cash, so it couldn't be traced, and pre-paid for calls. I would phone Hélène and ask her to book us in for two nights at the hotel, as it was obvious the Zürich sortie could not be accomplished within a day. I would fly over to the club, file a flight plan to Le Touquet, and fill the tanks. After arriving at Le Touquet, I would deceive the French with the same sightseeing ploy as before, and hopefully would not meet the local gendarme, or face Chief Bosenquet!

After our arrival at the farm, I asked Lu Ming to stay in the Bentley, while I told Louise we had a guest. He nodded and I hurried in to find my wife, who was in the kitchen cooking.

'Ah, you're just in time for dinner, and the kids are now in bed, thank heavens!'

'Is there enough for three?'

'What?'

'We have a guest, who will be staying the night.'

'...So, why didn't you call and tell me, for God's sake?'

'I was busy...'

'Do you think I'm a mind reader?' but before I could answer, she asked, 'so who is it?'

'...Lu Ming.'

Louise looked perplexed, and asked, 'I hope you are not getting yourself into more deep trouble, with this dreadful man?'

'No, I'm not, but I will be flying him to France tomorrow,' I replied.

'Peter… I just give up with you… you're worse than Roger!'

'Probably, my darling… I'll go and get him in,' I said with a smile, while Louise let out a gasp of desperation, shook her head, and raised her eyes to heaven.

Lu Ming was very polite from the start, and he complimented Louise on our meal of roast lamb. Afterwards, we went to the study, where I told him my plans for the next day. He seemed satisfied and said he would leave everything to me, before saying he was now tired, and wished to go to his room. I showed him upstairs, where he handed me fifty thousand pounds from the briefcase, for the disposal of his wife, saying, with a smile, he would keep the empty briefcase for the Swiss bearer bonds. I thanked him, and wished him 'goodnight,' before placing the cash, in a drawer, in our bedroom.

I went outside to phone Hélène, hoping she would be at 'Le Moulin Bleu.'

'Hello.'

'Hi Hélène … its Pierre!'

'Ah… Pierre, ma petite!' she replied excitedly.

'Oui, it's me… now, tomorrow I'm flying to Besancon with a friend…'

'A woman?' she interrupted.

'No, a gentleman who…'

'Ah très bien!' she interrupted.

'…Who you already know… it's Monsieur Lu Ming… and, we want to stay at 'Le Moulin Bleu'… so, will you book us in for two nights?'

'Of course, ma petite… what time will you land, so I can meet you?'

'…At about three, in the afternoon.'

'Bon, I'll be waiting at the airfield for you, Pierre.'

'Merci, Hélène … au revoir!'

'…Au revoir, ma petite!'

In bed that night, Louise and I had one of our 'whispered

discussions,' so as to not to wake the babes or Lu Ming. It became a little heated, when Louise questioned me closely about the trip to France… she was distinctly dissatisfied and nervous about the whole thing. We eventually went to sleep, and were not on good terms… but, we made up in the morning after the alarm went off, with lingering kisses and apologies.

After breakfast, I left Lu Ming in the kitchen sipping tea, and flew over to the club, where I paid my landing fee, and filed my flight plan with Phil, before Jimmy refuelled Papa Oscar. I landed back at the strip, and carried out one final check of the aircraft, before I went into the house for Lu Ming. He appeared a little anxious as we made our way to Papa Oscar, but said nothing.

Within minutes we were strapped in, and the engine started. I checked all systems, then opened the throttle, and within yards Papa Oscar lifted into the clear air… and, we were on our way to Besancon. I climbed to two thousand feet, reduced power to cruise, and trimmed out. The coast lay under my left wing, and it remained in that position until we reached Dover, where I called for a Channel crossing. After I received that, I turned Papa Oscar towards the French coast, and mid-Channel, I called French Air Traffic, at Pas de Calais, for clearance into Le Touquet. We landed soon afterwards, and Lu Ming remained in the aircraft, whilst I paid the landing fee, and advised the controller that I would be cruising around France sightseeing for a day or so. He seemed quite sanguine about that, and wished me, 'bon voyage.'

After departure, I set the course for Reims, and soon the cathedral appeared on the horizon, glistening in the sun. I constantly checked the heading to ensure I didn't wander off course, and miss the airfield at Besancon. Everything was in order, and at last the airfield came in sight. After calling the tower for landing instructions, which were given, I flew a circuit and lined Papa Oscar up with the runway, and touched down smoothly. I parked the aircraft and as we climbed from the cockpit, I saw Hélène running towards me.
    'Hello you!' I called, as she came closer.

'Oh, Pierre... Pierre, it's so good to see you!' she said, before flinging her arms around my neck, and kissing me passionately... well, the French are always a bit over enthusiastic!

When I was free from her embrace, I asked, 'you remember Monsieur Lu Ming?'

'Oui, of course, Pierre... how are you, monsieur?'

'Very well, thank you, mademoiselle,' he replied, with a smile.

'Bon... now mama has you booked in, so let's go, Pierre.'

After I paid the fee and told the controller I would leave Papa Oscar parked until tomorrow, before returning to the UK, we set off in Hélène's Renault to 'Le Moulin Bleu.'

Madame Dubois warmly welcomed us as we signed in, and Hélène showed us to our rooms. She followed me into mine, and said, 'I didn't think I'd ever see you again, Pierre.'

'Well, I always keep my promises, and told you I would come back,' I replied.

'I know... and, I'm so glad.'

'I'm pleased... and, it's lovely to see you again... now, I have a big favour to ask.'

'What is it, Pierre?'

'Will you drive us to Zürich tomorrow?'

'But, of course... I love a long drive... and it's so exciting in Papa's BMW!' she replied, enthusiastically.

'Will he mind?'

'Oh, non, Pierre... he lets me do anything I want!' she replied, before giving me a quick kiss on the cheek, and saying, 'dinner is at seven... don't be late!' And I laughed, as she flounced out!

Hélène joined us for dinner, which annoyed Lu Ming, as I suspected he wanted to talk... but I didn't care, as there was plenty of time to talk later, in his room. The meal was delicious, and even Lu Ming was impressed. After coffee, I asked Hélène if we could leave at nine in the morning, to which she readily agreed. We said 'goodnight' to her and went up to our rooms, where Lu Ming told me that he only expected to be in the bank for an hour, at the most. That suited me, as it meant we could return and spend one more night at the hotel, before flying home. Everything was now in place for a trouble-free journey, so I slept well.

We left the hotel at just after nine, and made good progress to the Swiss border. Hélène planned to stop at Luzern, for coffee and fuel, before a fast run to Zürich.

Lu Ming was pleased when we reached the outskirts of the picturesque city, and guided Hélène to the Credit Suisse Bank, in Heinrichstrasse. After she pulled up outside the bank, Lu Ming said, 'I will not be more than hour… so, go and have some coffee then come back.'
'We will, sir,' I replied, he gave a nod and climbed out, with his empty briefcase.
Hélène found a parking space close by, and we went in search of coffee and something to eat. Nearby was a little café, where we enjoyed Gruyère cheese rolls and several cups of coffee, before returning to the Bank. Lu Ming came out within minutes of our arrival; he smiled and climbed into the BMW, with his briefcase.
'All is well, Mr Cavendish… so, back to Besancon and then home to Britain!' he said, gleefully.
'Very good, sir… so, let's go Hélène!' And did she!

The drive back to 'Le Moulin Bleu' was more electrifying than terrifying, but we made it back safely. Although it was now quite late, Madam Dubois provided us with a delicious supper of boeuf bourguignon, followed by chocolate ice cream. We thanked her, before saying 'bonne nuit.' As we left the dining room, I whispered to Hélène, 'I've something for you in my room.'
Her eyes lit up, and she replied, 'I'll be with you in a few minutes, ma petite.' I nodded, and followed Lu Ming to the stairs, then up to our rooms. We said 'goodnight,' and he thanked me for a successful day… he had accomplished everything he wanted. In my room, I thought of the six million in Swiss bearer bonds, and wondered where I could hide the briefcase on the farm. My thoughts were interrupted by a knock at the door, and I opened it to a smiling Hélène. She entered, and asked coyly, 'so Pierre, what have you got for me?'
I went to my overnight bag, drew out a large brown envelope

and replied, 'this is for you, Hélène.'

'What is it?'

'There's two thousand pounds in here for you,' I replied, handing her the envelope.

She looked puzzled, and asked, 'but why... and, what for, Pierre?'

'Because I earned a good fee for flying Lu Ming here the last time... and, I wanted you to have some of it.'

'Oh, Pierre, ma petite, you are so kind...'

'Not at all, you deserve it for all you've done,' I interrupted, with a smile. Hélène slumped down the bed, opened the envelope, peered inside, looked at me, and said in a whisper, 'now let me do something for you!' I knew she meant sex, but quickly said, 'no, Hélène ...'

'Oh Pierre... please, please let me!'

'Hélène, I'm happily married, and cannot possibly let my wife down....'

'She is very lucky to have you, ma petite!' she interrupted.

'Possibly...'

'Don't you think I'm lovely and desirable?'

'Yes you are very beautiful, Hélène ... and, if I wasn't married, I'd...'

'Fuck me all night long!' she interrupted.

'...Exactly.'

'Well, I suppose that's good to know, ma petite... so, bonne nuit... and, you know I'm going to cry myself to sleep... I'll see you in the morning,' she said with passion, before leaving the room... and, I sighed.

Just after nine the next morning, Hélène drove us to the airfield, and after lingering kisses and several 'au revoirs,' I loaded our luggage into the sealed compartment in the fuselage behind the rear seats, and locked the hatch. As I climbed into the cockpit, it occurred to me that the luggage compartment might be an ideal place to keep the briefcase, until Lu Ming wanted it.

The return flight to Le Touquet, and then on to the farm was quite uneventful... for which I was grateful, as I'd had enough dramas recently! After landing, Lu Ming asked me once again to keep the bearer bonds safe for a week or so; as he would be in court for preliminary hearings, prior to a date being set for his trial. I promised I would, and guessed if things went badly for him, he would ask me to fly him into Europe again, so he could escape. We climbed out of Papa Oscar and went into the house, where a relieved Louise made sandwiches and some tea, before I drove him up to his house in Witney. Outside the mansion, we said 'goodbye,' shook hands, and he said he would call me when he wanted the bonds, which I would take to Grosvenor Square. He promised to pay me cash for my help, when I arrived.

A week passed with no call from Lu Ming, and I began to get concerned. The briefcase remained locked away in the luggage compartment, and I wondered if I should move it somewhere else, but decided it was safe there, so didn't bother.

A few days later my phone rang in the study. I thought was bound to be Lu Ming, but it was Morton calling from New Scotland Yard.

'Yes, Superintendent... what do you want this time?' I asked with a sigh.

'Do you know the whereabouts of Mrs Ming?' he asked, and shivers ran down my spine.

'No, I don't.'

'Hmm... are you sure, sir?'

'Yes quite sure, Superintendent,' I replied, truthfully.

'...Then perhaps you know the whereabouts of your friend Mr Roger Burton?'

'What's this all about, Superintendent?' I asked anxiously.

'Just answer the question if you please, sir.'

'No, I don't know where he is... and, now you'll please tell me what has happened?'

'Mr Lu Ming was found murdered, at his London home, this morning, sir...'

'Good God!' I whispered, and my mind ran riot with the possibilities of Roger's involvement.

'...And, we're anxious to trace his wife, sir.'

'Is she a suspect?'

'Mrs Ming needs to be informed of her husband's death, sir.'

'...Of course.'

'...And, when did you last have any contact with Mrs Ming?'

'I don't actually remember, but it was some time ago,' I replied truthfully.

'Now, when did you last see Roger Burton, sir?'

I gulped, and replied; 'it must have been a few weeks ago.'

'...And where was that, sir?'

'We met at the Randolph Hotel in Oxford.'

'...And what were you doing in Oxford, sir?'

'I was visiting my aunt at Yarnton, when Roger called and said he was staying at the Randolph, so we met up for a drink,' I replied.

'During your conversations, did he say where he was going after he left Oxford?'

'No, Superintendent, he didn't.'

'Are you absolutely sure about that, sir?'

'I'm quite sure.'

'Did he happen to mention Mrs Ming to you, sir?'

'Yes, he talked about her.'

'...And what did he say?'

'Well, only that he was friendly with her, and expected to be invited to her home in Witney, Superintendent.'

'Did he mention going away with Mrs Ming?'

'I don't think so, but I really can't remember,' I lied.

There was a short pause before Morton said, 'well, that'll be all for the moment, sir, but I will be in touch as the investigation develops... goodbye.'

'Goodbye, Superintendent.'

I was sweating as I replaced the phone, and wondered if Roger had murdered Lu Ming, or if it was one of the Chinese Government's assassins, that he feared.

I went back to the kitchen and told Louise.

'My God... do you think Roger did it?'

'I don't think so, but I really can't be sure... he's so unpredictable now,' I replied, before switching on the television and selecting BBC news. A serious-looking female presenter said, 'the prominent Chinese business man, Lu Ming, has been found dead at his London home by a maid. Apparently he had been shot while in the bath, and police are now anxious to trace his wife, who they think may be abroad at present. Mr Lu Ming was on police bail facing conspiracy charges from his business activities in Zürich, connected with the financing of arms dealing. We will bring you further information as soon as we get it.'

I switched the television off, looked at Louise, and said, 'what a bloody awful mess!'

She sighed, and replied, 'well at least he won't bother you anymore.'

'True... but, I wonder if there'll be a backlash.'

'Time will tell, darling.'

'...And, I've still got his Bearer Bonds!'

Paula phoned soon after she had seen the television coverage on the murder, and asked what I knew about it. I told her nothing that hadn't already been reported, and she said that she would like to come and stay for a few days. I welcomed the idea that Paula would be here to discuss anything that might come up... she was my rock.

Paula arrived the next day, just after Natasha had called, and asked if I had killed Lu Ming. I told her not to be so silly, and I asked if she had been surprised at his murder.

'No not really, darling... he obviously had made many enemies,' she replied.

'I suppose you're glad that you didn't move into his flat then?'

'Well, I wasn't about to give up Tim and Chris without a struggle, and a big financial inducement,' she replied, I laughed and thought, 'sex and money make the world go around!'

We said our 'goodbyes,' and promised to keep in touch.

Over dinner and drinks, Louise and I discussed the situation with Paula, and I told her about the bearer bonds. She looked surprised, and gave us her carefully thought-out advice, which was to do nothing, until something happened, before we eventually went up to bed. The next day I tried to call Roger's mobile twice, but it went dead each time. It was obvious that he really didn't want to be contacted, not even by me. I was very sad that it had all come to this… but, life goes on… relentlessly.

I suggested that we should all go on holiday to our villa in Cassis, Louise was delighted and Paula said that we all deserved a break. At the end of the week, I phoned Morton to ask if the investigation had any major developments, to which he replied, 'we're making steady progress, Mr Cavendish.'
  'I'm pleased to hear it… now I must inform you that I'm going away for two weeks… I'll be staying with my family at our villa in France, but you can reach me on my mobile if you need to.'
  'Thank you for keeping me informed, sir.'

On the Sunday, we packed the twins and everything else into the Bentley and set off for the South of France. As I drove on the AutoRoute, south of Paris towards Nemours, I thought of Hélène … I planned to fly over, with Louise, to Besancon, to see her once again, and give her another reward. I looked forward to flying in the snow-covered French Alps with the lovely, talented young woman, and I was sure that Louise would like her.

At our villa, we enjoyed two weeks of sublime bliss, drinking too much wine, eating too much delicious food, putting on weight, and swimming naked in the pool each day. I was sad to leave, as it had been such a good, restful holiday for us all. On our return, I checked that the briefcase, locked away in Papa Oscar, was still there, with its six million pounds worth of Credit Suisse bearer bonds… and, it was… while wondering what I should do now!

I decided to follow Paula's advice, and leave it until I had more time to think, or something happened. The same advice was followed regarding Lu Ming's ex-wives… I didn't really want to go to Beijing. I often wondered if he had murdered Leisha… or was it a dreadful accident as he claimed. You rarely know the truth about anybody, do you?

Just over a month passed with no contact from Morton, or my

solicitor, or the Americans... so, I assumed everything was now in order, and I was no longer under any suspicion regarding Lu Ming's murder, or his business activities in Zürich... then one evening Roger phoned me from Hong Kong!

         THE END
                  ……… well, I hope it is!

Lightning Source UK Ltd.
Milton Keynes UK
UKOW05f0105210317
297120UK00004B/5/P